About the Author

Robert has been writing since he was a child and actually wanted to be a rock star. He's got the hair and the guitar, but has also managed to be many other things. He decided to write children's books so that he can put all of his favourite things into one place – animals, magic and silly jokes.
He also thinks that snails have an agenda…

To Nicky

Toad

Thanks for not
giving up on
me and keeping
me going.

Robert

Robert Davidson

Toad

Olympia Publishers
London

www.olympiapublishers.com
OLYMPIA PAPERBACK EDITION

A CIP catalogue record for this title is
available from the British Library.

ISBN: 978-1-80439-720-6

This is a work of fiction.
Names, characters, places and incidents originate from the writer's
imagination. Any resemblance to actual persons, living or dead, is
purely coincidental. (Although some of the animals are based on the
author's former pets) No magic was used on any animals or humans in
the writing of this book.

First Published in 2024

Olympia Publishers
Tallis House
2 Tallis Street
London
EC4Y 0AB

Printed in Great Britain

Dedication

This book is dedicated to Alan, the cat, a true legend missed to this day.

Acknowledgements

Thank you to all at Olympia Publishing, for taking a chance on me and letting my dream come true. Thanks to Sir Terry, for the inspiration. And thank you to YOU, for taking the time to read what has come out of my head.

One

The Toad jumped. He knew it wasn't far, but with the rain coming down (and Toad being very scared) he still worried about the landing. He closed his eyes and hoped that he did not become a flat green splodge down below.

When he heard a loud *plosh* Toad realised he wasn't dead. He opened his eyes and saw that he was sitting on a patch of grass. In a puddle. He was in the open air.

He was out!

Toad had been trapped for over a hundred years. He thought for a moment – knowing his luck, it had probably been longer. Turning round, he looked at what had been his prison. Walls made from old stone, framed by old wooden beams, with a slate tile roof. It looked much smaller on the outside than he remembered it. Toad found it almost impossible that he had spent the last century (possibly longer, as said earlier) in that small cottage, copying, translating and preparing scrolls for his captor.

Being a toad that could read, write and play a variety of musical instruments had its advantages. But it also brought problems, such as not being able to reach the pedals on a piano. There had been nothing to play in the cottage; no trumpet, no harp. Not even a recorder (and who wants to play that anyway?).

Toad rubbed his leg where it ached. There were still a few sores from being chained to a desk. He has used his writing quill to unlock the latch on his shackles. It had been a good idea. To be fair, Toad thought, it had taken him twelve years to pick the lock (the quill kept snapping). But now he was out, and time was important. He had to warn everyone about the children…

A wailing cry from behind him reminded Toad that he was not safe yet. He looked around. Through the hammering rain the trees around the cottage reached up to the dark sky, making Toad think that he was being watched, and not by something pleasant.

Toad stretched his stumpy legs and ran forward as quickly as he could, making little splashing sounds as his bulky body hit the rainwater in the grass. As he reached the trees that horrible cry came again. Toad stopped and took a glance at the cottage.

A bright orange glow lit up the cottage from inside. The light danced through the blackening windows as the flames within slowly ate through the wooden panels and window sills. Toad allowed himself a smile. His captor couldn't escape that!

Glass shattered everywhere as a huge, black furry shape rocketed through one of the windows. It landed on the damp grass, steam rising from slightly charred fur. Something that looked like a head slowly scanned around. Toad quivered as he caught a glimpse of two pale green eyes looking at the trees. Where he was. Within those eyes Toad believed he saw pain and anger. He was sure that he could not be seen, yet just to look at those eyes was enough to freeze him to the spot. Toad felt wet soil seep between his toes. He had been here too long.

Toad backed slowly into the trees, keeping an eye on

the smouldering heap of fur. It didn't move. Toad allowed himself to breathe out. The ears of the dark creature pricked up. One had a bit missing from the tip. Toad hoped that the animal hadn't heard him breathe.

'TOAD!'

The animal roared with a voice that didn't belong in such a small creature. The sound carried across the grass and Toad felt as though he had been poked in the eye as a result. He watched as the creature started to claw its way across the wet grass like a puppet that had had its strings cut.

Toad gave up.

He ran.

As a toad, he was not very tall. Toads, as a rule, generally aren't. Add this to the fact that Toad was in woodland at night with rain slashing down and who-knows-what kind of evil after him, he felt very small.

From what he could remember, there were some houses to the east of here. If he could reach them and hide somewhere then at least he could think about what he had to do. Toad thought about who he knew and how many of his old friends would still be around and, more importantly, who would actually help him. A particularly big raindrop splashed onto Toad's head. Stars appeared before his eyes and he nearly blacked out. It was like being slapped by an elephant. A big one. Toad shook his bulbous head to clear his vision. He had to keep moving!

The rain and muddy ground made Toad's journey difficult. This wasn't helped by occasional tree roots sticking up (on purpose, Toad felt) and getting in his way. Toad did stop for a snack though. There were some flies buzzing around a small pile of rabbit poo and he couldn't resist. He rubbed his belly after eating (the flies, not the poo), feeling satisfied. Toad hadn't eaten for a very long time. In fact, he could not remember the last time he had eaten. He began to wonder if he had actually eaten anything for over a century. Then he remembered; he hadn't. And to Toad's annoyance, he had not lost any weight at all!

There was no path, not really – just mud and puddles now that cut through the trees. A movement reflected in a puddle nearby made Toad spin round, hastily looking this way and that. Toad couldn't be sure, but he felt that something was following him. Something definitely *not nice*. There. Over near the fallen tree trunk, covered with moss and toadstools. Movement again. Something...*green*...

Then it was gone. Toad tried to slow his breathing down. It had been like staring at an eye blinking. A bright, haunting, green eye. Toad crawled away, turning round every twenty paces or so just to check that it wasn't something terribly horrible hunting him wanting to eat his brain.

It had stopped raining now. The night air had started to warm up again, the only water falling now just drops from rain-soaked leaves high up in the trees. Smells were clearer. Toad could detect the scent of woodland flowers, dingy mushrooms and also the rabbit poo where he had dined earlier. He could also smell...*danger*?

Toad looked around again. The wind had woken up, sending a breeze wafting through the trees towards where Toad was sitting. It also brought the stink of *evil*...

Two

Toad ran from the trees as fast as he could. The casual observer would liken Toad's attempt at running to an out-of-control ping pong ball. Houses were ahead of him. Toad picked the nearest one and started pacing round the back fence, searching for a hole in the wooden planks or a gap between the fence and the soil that he could squeeze through.

Toad even considered jumping over the fence, but not having had much practice at that sort of thing for over a hundred years meant that was one hop too far. He could build himself up to that sort of jump slowly (when he had some time off). Toad decided that if he had time tomorrow he would start getting back into shape by jumping over local snails. Snails were good for that sort of thing. Their shells were a decent height for hopping practice and they didn't move very fast (which meant they couldn't chase after you if they were annoyed by you using them as a hurdle).

Toad finally found a large enough gap under the fence for him to wriggle through. Just over halfway in, Toad realised that his hind quarters (otherwise known as his large bottom) were bigger than he remembered. There was a slight crack as the rotten wood of the fence gave way and Toad was thrown face first into the waterlogged soil of the garden. He raised his muddy head. He noticed two snails nearby patiently watching him.

"Evening," Toad said hurriedly, pretending not to be embarrassed, then picking himself up and scrabbling through the garden towards the house. The snails glanced at each other and shrugged, shells quivering in amusement. Snails don't say much about what they find funny, and no one has ever commented on how snails laugh. They do laugh, though. But they're not saying how. One idea, cooked up by a local hedgehog, is that snails hypnotise you with their antennae; this means you forget facts about snails (This would have been a great theory if the hedgehog in question could remember why he thought about it in the first place).

Toad reached the end of the lawn and stared up at the house. Unclimbable bricks stared back. Large windows on the ground floor let slivers of light filter through cracks in the curtains. Toad sat there, blinking. Then it came to him. He would have snapped his fingers if his feet weren't webbed. The drainpipe!

Toad tottered over to the drainpipe fixed over the grid. He looked it up and down, from the water trickling out of the bottom to the leaf-cluttered gutter at the top. Toad stretched his limbs and crawled into the drainpipe, brushing aside the leaves and grime that had collected at the bottom of the pipe. He managed to get all of his toady bulk inside and examined the surroundings. The pipe was cleaner than Toad thought it would be. This was not altogether a good thing; however, as Toad would have difficulty scaling the smooth plastic of the pipe without some dirt to cling on to. Still, it had to be done.

Toad stuck out his arms and legs and used his bulk to slowly (*very* slowly) ease himself up the pipe. The problem was that as his body was blocking the pipe as he climbed, any rainwater running into the pipe was collecting around his head. Toad could feel the water trickling around his bottom, but it wasn't trickling fast enough.

He was lucky that he was amphibious and used to water.

After what seemed like another century, Toad poked his gasping head out of the drainpipe, causing a jet of water to shoot up as though the pipe was a plastic dolphin spouting its blowhole. He gripped the rim of the pipe and stayed there for a moment, catching his breath. The slate of the roof was just ahead of him. Toad pulled himself out of the pipe with a loud 'pop'. He looked back down to where he had climbed from. On the lawn in the garden below, the snails were watching him still, bobbing their antennae in appreciation. Yep, it had been a truly heroic climb. All that was needed now was a small, simple jump to get onto the roof.

He leapt...and caught.

His back legs dangling, Toad put all the strength he could into pulling himself up onto the slate above. Dragging his head above the tile – he found himself looking directly into a pair of fierce, amber eyes set into a ginger and white furry face. There was a scar running across the nose, just between those eyes, and the whiskers attached to the face were bristling with irritation.

"You know, with just one poke I could create history's first flying Toad!" the cat said calmly.

"Er...hello Alan," Toad said, almost forgetting that he was hanging over a drop that would leave him all over the place (well bits of him anyway). The cat leaned forward and stretched out a paw, the claws appearing slowly, and slightly touching Toad's worried face. Toad was sure that Alan (the cat – see above) was trying not to smile. Which worried him. Toad's back legs were flapping around behind, trying to find some grip on the bricks and stop him from falling.

"Explain yourself Toad!"

"After a hundred years," Toad gasped, starting to panic, his front legs slipping, "all you can do is threaten?" Alan watched Toad slip backwards then thrust out his paw further.

"Grab hold," he said, putting his claws back in, "I'll pull you up." Toad gripped Alan's outstretched foreleg and held on tight. Alan didn't even flinch as he lifted Toad up and placed the amphibian next to him on the tiles. The cat watched Toad for a moment through narrowed eyes as Toad gathered himself together and calmed down.

"Right. Now tell me what's going on and why you are here!" Toad looked Alan straight in the eyes. Alan raised an eyebrow, waiting for an answer. Toad opened his mouth to speak, closed it, shuffled his feet on the damp tiles then replied.

"When was the last time you saw me?" he asked. Alan shrugged. "Also, let me ask you what *you* are doing *here*, on this roof?" Alan scratched on the tiles with a lazy claw.

"I live here."

"What? With the humans?"

"Yes. Why? What's wrong with me getting free food and having a place to sleep?" Toad looked at the open bedroom window and then back at Alan.

"Are they aware that you are eight hundred and eighty-six years old?"

Three

Toad knew that Alan would not have given anything away to the humans, but he still had to ask. He had been away too long. Toad looked at his muddy feet.

"Sorry," he said quietly, "I'm having a bit of a rough night."

"What problems have you brought with you?" Alan asked, lying down on his side and idly flicking his tail. He glanced at Toad and then out at the darkness of the garden and the woodland beyond. "Or can I guess?"

"Has anything…strange happened recently?" Toad asked quietly.

"Strange?"

Stranger than normal. Alan thought for a moment. He shook his furry head. Toad frowned. "Are you sure?" Toad pressed, forgetting just how big Alan actually was. Then again, he was not a normal cat.

"No. Nothing. The mice have not been active for years," Alan said, scratching his stomach. Toad walked right up to Alan so that his knobbly green-brown face almost touched the cat's pink nose.

"I don't mean with the animals. I mean with the humans." Alan stopped scratching. He sat up now.

"Well…"

"Yes?"

"Children have been going missing," Alan said quietly,

"and they are all local to this area. But I didn't think that was our business." Toad nodded.

"Usually it wouldn't be." Toad shuffled uneasily. "But things have changed." What he was about to say could land him in a massive heap of trouble. "We need to break the bond." Alan was very quiet. He stood up, shaking his head, towering over Toad. "Shadow is ready to act." That did it. Just hearing the name of his old enemy was enough to make the cat extend his claws. Toad looked at the tile beneath Alan's paws. "You're digging in with your claws, by the way."

"How long have you known?" Alan asked through gritted teeth.

"About your claws, or Shadow?"

"*Don't joke with me!*" Alan yelled, punching the slate tiles so hard that one cracked. Toad hopped back, knowing that he had made one funny remark too many. The cracked tile started crumbling, proof for Toad that even after all these years Alan's immense strength had not faded. "We should get inside." Turning his back on Toad he jumped onto the window sill of the open window, disappearing inside. Alan poked his head out. "Coming?" he asked, "or should I leave you there?"

Toad made his way across the tiles. He looked up at the open window and sighed. Another jump! It was hard to get a decent grip on the tiles with his feet. He heard the sound of a cat sighing and muttering to itself before a ginger and white furry arm appeared from the window above. Toad leapt and grabbed hold of Alan's foreleg for the second time that night and tried to relax as Alan pulled him on to the window sill.

Toad gave the room a quick glance. A child's bedroom. Model cars and spaceships were arranged neatly on a shelf in one corner, whilst on the other side of the room a tall bookshelf was crammed full of reading material ranging from comics to encyclopaedias. A chart of the solar system adorned one wall, 'Flags of The World' on a colourful poster next to it. The big clue as to it being a child's bedroom, however, was the young boy sleeping peacefully in the bed near the window.

"Who's he?" Toad asked, whispering his question so that he didn't wake the boy.

"That's Eric," Alan replied, "now get off the window sill and get out of sight!" Toad considered his journey off the window sill. A straight leap onto the floor (he guessed about a metre) would be okay but, Toad admitted, with his bulk the noise when he landed would not be a small 'plop'. No, he needed to find another route. There was a chest of drawers next to the bed, that would do for a start. The jump required wasn't much easy, or it would have been if Toad had remembered that he had muddy feet...

Toad's feet hit the edge of the chest of drawers and instead of landing safely (and with style) he felt himself fall backwards towards the carpet. There was a 'thump'. Toad didn't move.

"Idiot!" Alan cursed.

"I'm fine, thanks," Toad retorted, "thanks for asking." He began rolling himself from side to side in order to get the right way up again.

Alan watched the boy. Eric stirred slightly but didn't wake up. Alan breathed a sigh of relief. He then turned his attention to Toad and his efforts to look dignified with his legs in the air and his belly exposed to the ceiling. Alan was glad that the boy had not woken. He could think of better ways of breaking the Bond than having a human discover a cat and a toad arguing in the darkness at two in the morning. Alan padded over to where Toad was finally on his feet again instead of on his back. He pointed under the bed, "Stay tonight. We'll decide what to do tomorrow." Toad nodded, dragging himself wearily towards the darkness underneath the bed. He was lucky there was enough room (although he had not been under many beds before and so to Toad this was an adventure). Alan stopped him by putting a massive paw on Toad's shoulder. "Hang on," he said, pulling Toad back from the bed. "We... need to do something first." Alan looked awkward for a moment before continuing. "I...well, look...it's not as though you haven't been through worse."

"What?"

"I need to wee on you."

"Say that again?"

"Look, you need to smell like a cat...if the other animals round here pick up the scent of toad, then they'll get suspicious!"

"I'll take the risk, thanks!"

"Also, if you've got Shadow after you, then surely it's the best thing to put him off?" Toad considered this. After nearly killing Shadow when he started the cottage fire earlier tonight he didn't think that Shadow would be seeking him out to give him a cuddle (maybe one with claws and a bit of death). Toad gave in. He nodded.

Toad closed his eyes as Alan cocked his leg, then he felt a warm trickle on his head that ran down his back.

"Done," Alan said, and Toad suspected Alan had enjoyed that. He spent a few undignified moments letting his unwelcome shower dry so that the scent would cling to him and then crawled under the bed. *What a night!*

Four

Eric was a boy. He had average looks, an above-average level of intelligence and wasn't interested in playing games. What he did have was a greater than average level of common sense. Eric was one of those people who *dealt* with situations. Thinking carefully. Weighing up options. Then coming up with a way to solve the problem that should have been obvious to everyone else if they bothered to think properly.

Eric was also late for school.

Despite his other abilities, Eric's time keeping was, to be fair, rubbish. The problem was that he could always find something more interesting to do than, say, go downstairs when called for dinner. Reading a book about the Middle Ages or watching a television show about how engines work was more important. After all, he could always make a sandwich later if he was hungry.

Eric bent to tie his shoelaces and noticed a faint brown stain on his bedroom carpet – right near the window. Eric frowned as he thought about this. The stain hadn't been there last night. He finished with his laces and looked briefly at Alan, who was at that moment asleep on the windowsill. That was another thing. Eric was sure that he had opened the window before he had gone to bed last night.

Eric did what he normally did when faced with a

puzzle. Without blinking Eric looked around his room, as if he was a camera or scanning for interesting data. He took all the information in and considered it in seconds. The most logical explanation was that Alan had closed the window. But cats don't do that. Eric had never found any evidence saying that cats (or any pets) did things like that at random. It also didn't explain the brown stain on the carpet. Looking closer at Alan Eric couldn't see any mud on the slumbering cat's paws.

Frowning, Eric picked up his school bag and was nearly at his bedroom door when he noticed the smell. It was…wee. But Eric was sure that it wasn't him. He hadn't done anything like that in his bedroom for years (apart from one time last autumn when he had a nightmare, but we won't talk about that).

A ginger movement caught his eye. Eric looked over at the waking shape of Alan.

"Morning," Eric said, nodding at the cat as Alan jumped off the window sill and padded towards him. "Shut the window, did you?" Eric joked. He was sure that Alan looked at him with a guilty expression for a moment before that cat walked around Eric's legs and rubbed his fur against Eric's ankles. Eric bent and tickled Alan under the chin.

"What do you get up to at night, Alan?" Eric asked, ruffling the fur on Alan's head before leaving. Alan watched him go.

There was a new boy in Eric's class. He was introduced as Shane, and had moved to the area only recently. Shane waved at everyone and found a seat near the back of the class.

Shane was a little bit smaller than Eric, and had a mass of untidy black hair that nearly reached his shoulders. His skin was pale and he had a thin mouth and nose that seemed to twitch every now and then. That was it – apart from his eyes…Eric noticed that they were a piercing green that almost seemed *too* green (if that was possible).

As the day went on, the other thing Eric realised was that Shane did not speak much, and when he did he gave short answers. To Eric it seemed as though Shane didn't really want to be there and *really* hated people talking to him. Eric actually found Shane a bit creepy. It was the smile. Shane had a habit of looking away from his classmates smiling to himself when they were speaking to him. Everyone else thought Shane was funny. Eric wasn't so sure.

During break the boys passed the time by kicking a ball around. Eric joined in; mainly because he was bored (he *would* allow himself to play a game now and then as long as it did not get in the way). Shane sat by himself on a bench nearby, watching the boys with an amused look on his face. Once or twice one of the other boys would ask Shane if he wanted to join in but he just shook his head and waved them away.

The game was almost over when Eric passed the ball to Mickey, who, having more meat in his right leg than Eric had in his entire body, kicked the ball so hard that it rocketed over everyone's head and blasted into the trees nearby. Everyone groaned. Someone punched Mickey on the arm and Eric heard someone else actually say 'idiot'.

"Well done," Eric said, breathing heavily after running around. "That's the game over."

Eric felt a hand on his shoulder' He turned quickly, startled. Shane was looking straight at him with those green eyes. That smile was still there too.

"I'll get it," Shane said, nodding his head towards the trees. There were a few shouts along the line of 'don't be daft!' and 'you'll never get up there!' followed by shaking of heads and laughing. Eric looked at the tree. It seemed impossible to climb. A thick grey trunk that looked like a wrinkly grape and a mass of twisted branches. Shane stopped at the base of the tree, looking up into the branches. The laughing carried on behind him. It stopped very quickly.

With unbelievable skill and speed Shane leapt onto the tree and made his way into the branches. *How was he doing it?* The boys had tried to climb this tree before and there were many stories of the injuries they had got from trying! They all stood open mouthed as Shane crawled between the branches towards the ball.

The boys looked at each other in disbelief. It was as though they were all under some kind of spell. All of this ended rather suddenly with a loud 'pop' followed by a hissing sound. There was a noise like a low growl above them. The boys looked at the ground where their ball now lay, shrinking, shrivelling slowly as the air escaped from it.

"Caught on a branch," Shane's voice from above. Eric was about to say that it didn't matter when all speech was shocked out of him as Shane jumped down from the branches, roll and land on his feet in a crouch. Shane stood up and wiped his clothes down. There were patches of green, brown and grey from brushing against the tree. And as he walked past the boys he was still smiling…

Later the teacher gathered the class for a talk. The children all sat there, wondering what was going on. She stood up nervously.

"Er. Right. You know that some local children have...gone missing?" There were nods and 'yes' responses. In one case, crying (there's always one). "Please be careful as Penny Silverman has disappeared." With that, the teacher hurried everyone home. Penny was a year younger than Eric. He didn't know her very well, but she lived near the church nearby, about ten minutes from his house.

On his way out of the door, Eric caught sight of Shane. Still smiling...

Five

Alan was about to lick his paw yet again but stopped himself. Toad had noticed Alan doing that and decided it must be a habit of the large cat.

"Three missing," Alan said seriously, "so far."

"So far?"

"Think about it. If this is the work of Shadow then I doubt he'll stop soon." Alan paused, then added, "Whatever it is he wants."

Toad padded around Eric's bedroom, examining the posters on the walls and the books on display. He frowned.

"Does this boy have any toys?"

"No," Alan replied grumpily, settling down for a nap.

"What kind of boy has no toys?" a mumbled grunt from Alan. "A boy who reads books instead of plays!"

"He's got model cars."

"Oh!" Toad sidled over to the lounging cat and tapped Alan softly on his white and ginger head. A very angry amber eye slid open.

"What?"

"Er…any chance of some food?"

Eric opened the door to his house and paused. Something seemed odd. He felt as though he was being watched. Slowly, he looked round, trying to spot anything out of the ordinary. Apart from two snails next to the doorstep there was nothing. Eric laughed. And the snails wouldn't, be watching him, would they?

He walked into the hall and dumped his school bag on the chair by the stairs, letting the front door shut behind him. Carrying on into the kitchen Eric spent five minutes making himself a cheese sandwich before heading upstairs to his bedroom.

Eric almost dropped his sandwich as he opened his bedroom door, looking at a rather large (and smelly) toad sitting next to Alan who were both looking back at Eric. Just for a minute Eric thought they looked…guilty.

The toad nudged Alan with a stubby foreleg and tilted its head at Eric. Alan shook his head in turn and nodded at the toad. Eric stood there. Nothing usually bothered him, and he couldn't say that this did. However, he didn't know what was going on and that *was* something that he didn't like.

Eric considered this, (he felt that anyone else would scream *"Get that toad out of my bedroom!"* but after some thought Eric came to the conclusion that 'something' was happening). He sat on his bed, facing the odd pair.

"What is it, Alan?" Eric said softly, carefully picking a large crumb from his sandwich and nibbling on it. There was another nudge from the toad to the cat.

"Don't be afraid, boy," the toad said, raising its forelegs in a calming gesture. Eric didn't reply (usually at this point people run off, but as we said, Eric thinks differently). "We don't talk to humans, not allowed to, but… this is a time when we need to work together to stop the evil that is at work!" (A crash of thunder would have been fantastic here).

Eris sat for a moment, quietly munching on his sandwich. Toad thought it looked like a really *good* sandwich. The two animals looked at each other again, then back at Eric. Eric put the sandwich on his bed and walked to his collection of books. He glanced briefly at Toad then back to the books. Eric picked one.

"Shouldn't he be asking why we can talk?" Toad whispered to Alan, not taking his eyes from Eric. Alan said nothing, simply licked his paw again. Opening the book named *Amphibians* Eric sat in front of the pair, flicking the pages thoughtfully. He stopped at a certain point and turned the book round so that Toad and Alan could see what he had been reading. It was a highly coloured photograph of a toad. It was similar to our Toad.

"You're a Colorado River Toad," said Eric, turning the book back so he could read it. "It says here if someone licks you or tries to eat you, they see things that aren't there." Eric closed the book with a 'snap' and sat there looking thoughtful. "So how did you end up here in England?"

"So, you're not bothered that you have talking animals in your bedroom," Alan stated, not quite understanding.

"Makes sense, I suppose," Eric replied, putting the book back and sitting cross-legged on the floor. "I assume you've always been able to talk?"

"Well…there wasn't a need to talk to humans for hundreds of years. The last people who did were…kind of…burnt for being witches."

"And how many were they?" (Eric asks a lot of questions)

"Some," Toad replied, scratching his belly, "and that's part of the problem. In order to protect the humans, we had

31

to stop talking to them."

"Did it work?" (Eric found this all very interesting, but he still had to know)

"Well…" Toad was going to speak but Alan got there before him, "people carried on talking to animals who didn't talk back and there were a lot of bonfires."

Six

School was boring. Eric knew all the answers (nothing new and everyone knew he knew). The day went slowly. Eric didn't care about numbers, words, and games; he wanted to get back home and talk to his new friends.

Shane was strange. Again. The nickname 'Strange Shane' had started to be used by some of the other children. Whether Shane heard or not, he didn't seem to care. He just sat in class and smiled.

"Why does he have to smile like that?" Robin muttered as he walked home with Eric. Robin was a small boy with tight curly red hair and freckles (there's a child like that in every school). He was 'That Kid' (the one with all the freckles and won't share them).

"*Hmm*?" Eric wasn't really listening.

"Shane!" Robin shrieked. He made up for his lack of height with energy and a band temper.

"Oh. Right." Eric didn't look up.

"He smiles that smile and doesn't say much. Like he's just watching us all the time and laughing!"

"Maybe he is," Eric replied, deciding to steer Robin in a sensible direction for thinking. Eric knew that if Robin was left to his own opinion then he would walk right up to Shane and ask him – Eric didn't know why, but he felt that this would not be a good idea for Robin. There was indeed something about Shane that said 'danger'. Everyone else thought he was odd, but Eric thought that Shane projected a 'wrongness' about him. "He's new, that's all," Eric said, giving Robin his most reasonable look. Robin went quiet. Eric knew Robin was thinking. Robin's mouth hung slightly open when he was thinking. Eric believed that one day a fly would land in there and make a home.

"Yeah, maybe." Robin had come to a decision. Eric sighed. "But why does he have to smile?"

Eric waited in the darkness. His parents went to be. Eric moved an hour later. Toad had been a problem; Eric didn't know that toads could snore (it wasn't in any book he'd read). Alan had shoved Toad into Eric's wardrobe so that the sound was softened.

"Let's get Toad and go," Eric whispered to Alan as he carefully pulled the wardrobe door open. Eric looked in the wardrobe and then at Alan. "Why is he tied up with a sock in his mouth?"

Alan licked a paw. "Just in case." The cat cut through the shoelace he had secured Toad with and pulled the sock out of Toad's mouth. Toad glared at Alan from the darkness of the wardrobe.

"Not. Happy."

"So, what now?" Eric asked, avoiding the vacuum cleaner that his dad had left on the landing. Toad waddled in the direction of the kitchen.

"First, we eat."

Eric could cope with darkness. This was a good thing, as it was the middle of the night. He didn't mind the cold either (another good thing, as it was also cold). He did struggle with rain (there was a lot of this). Sudden downpours are, well, sudden, and so Eric was caught in a shower as he left his back garden and went into the woods with the cat and the toad.

The patter of rain on leaves was loud, the ground under Eric's feet became softer, muddier, and is best described by the word 'squelchy'. What did cheer Eric up was when he saw Alan drenched right through. Rain trickled from his whiskers in a mini waterfall as his fur became matted and clogged with dirt. Eric asked his friends how far they had to go as he stepped over a puddle that five minutes before had been a hole (and home to several ants, two earthworms and there were rumours that a hedgehog used it as a spare bedroom when his mum visited).

"The problem is," Toad said, "we're looking for a certain tree." Eric nodded. "But this tree doesn't always stay where you saw it last." Eric stopped squelching but still managed to put his foot in another puddle.

"He means that you could find the tree in one place then come back the next day and it will be somewhere else," Alan added.

"Ah, right. What?" Eric had a new feeling. It was called confusion. Taking a deep breath, he replied, "Trees. Do. Not. Move."

"Not usually," Toad said, looking up at the tree trunks that appeared black in the darkness. "Unless there's something interesting going on. Or they're running away from something." Eric took a deeper breath.

"Trees. Do. Not. Move." Eric looked at the others, who were both staring up above them. Being less than two feet tall (seven inches in Toad's case), this was something they did a lot.

"Trees are not really what you think they are," Toad said as though standing in front of a class teaching people who *really don't get it*. "The idea of a tree is something humans thought of." Eric's confusion increased (more new experiences for Eric). "Trees are more like animals. They have personalities, feelings, and know damn well when humans are watching."

"Surely not!" Eric wasn't convinced.

"Wait until you've lost an argument with a tree, is all I'm saying," Toad finished. Eric looked around at the trees surrounding them. "So, don't do anything to embarrass yourself. Trees have long memories and will talk about that silly human long after you've been dead."

Eric was going through a lot of new experiences tonight, and he was proud of how he was coping. Only yesterday he had learned that animals could talk (and live for hundreds of years), that some of these animals were trying to protect him and (more worryingly), some may be trying to kill him (or someone else, which is not as bad depending on who it is). Now he was in the company of a toad and a cat on a very dark (and wet, let's not forget that) night and looking for a certain tree (which may or may not be there or exist).

Seven

Eric wasn't scared; he was 'interested', which kind of masks fear in a weird way. This was better than going to school and doing homework (whoops! He'd forgotten that tonight). Even if there was the possibility of him getting into trouble or maybe even dying (from the events tonight, not his homework). He was lost in these thoughts when he nearly stepped on Toad, who had stopped suddenly.

Eric moved his foot away from Toad's head and set it down. He looked around him. Toad raised a foreleg, pointing to a small group of trees nearby.

"Maybe there?" Eric looked from those trees to some of the other trees. Then some others. He gave up. There was a big tree theme here. They all appeared to be the same.

"How can you tell?"

"They feel different."

"*Feel* different?"

"Just go with it."

Alan pattered forward, sniffing, then speeding up into a trot before leaping onto the nearest tree. Eric and Toad watched as Alan dug his claws into the bark of the tree and clambered up, breathing hard as he went higher. After a few seconds, Alan shook his head and jumped to the next tree, climbing up and down, poking with a claw, sniffing here and there at the damp wood. Another shake of his furry head. A jump to another tree.

Eric realised that this could take a while. He let his gaze wander around the trees surrounding the area. He almost missed it. One tree didn't look, well, 'right'. About halfway up the trunk, the bark seemed too smooth. It was almost like a face. Eric went to the tree, his steps squelching again as he moved.

As he got closer, Eric could make out more details – shapes appeared to him; lots of little triangles packed together, two big circles, another triangle, bigger than the others. The circles were eyes. *The triangles were feathers…so the last triangle must be a beak?*

Eric realised that he was staring at an image of an owl, looking as though it had been carved into the bark of the tree. He had been into the woods many times over the years, and never noticed this. In fact, for a boy who prided himself on his amazing memory and ability to spot clues, solve puzzles and explain things to others, he felt like a bit of a buffoon.

Then the owl blinked…

Eric made a noise. He hadn't made a noise like that before. It was a bit of a surprise to Toad and Alan as well as Eric. If he had to describe the noise to someone who hadn't heard it, Eric would have to say that it sounded something like *ooeeerrkahburah*.

Later, Toad admitted that he *may* have had a little wee in panic.

Alan and Toad followed Eric's gaze up the tree to where the owl was. Or where it had been. Eric blinked. Where had it gone?

"Excuse me?" said a voice like chestnuts being crunched together. "What day is it?"

Eric and the animals turned slowly (with a lot of squelching, still) and looked up to where the voice had come from.

There was no mistake. It was an owl. A wooden owl. No, not a *wooden* owl, an owl *made* from the wood! On a low branch, wings made of thin bark folded behind it, the owl glared at them with large eyes made of dark oak.

Eric was sure that those wooden eyes were looking *into* him, as though they were searching for a secret that he had hidden within. The beak (which appeared to be made of two halves of an acorn) moved.

"I don't like asking questions twice," it said, tilting its head to the side; all the while the owl still did not take its eyes off Eric.

"Er…Thursday?" Toad volunteered, because, well, *why not?* The owl looked away from Eric and up to the sky.

"No. That will not do. I do not like Thursday."

"Sunday?" Eric suggested, because, as Toad thought, why not?

"No. Sunday is not helpful," the owl said.

"What day would you like it to be?" Eric asked, feeling that this could possibly take a while. Then the owl was gone. Eric blinked.

"Wednesday. I've always liked Wednesday," said a voice near his knee. Eric looked down at the owl. It was quite clear that the owl was able to move around a) very quickly so that you didn't see it move or b) (which would take some deep thinking) that the owl was magical and do things Eric thought were impossible. To be fair, Eric thought calmly, I've recently met a talking toad, and learned that my cat has been keeping secrets from humans for hundreds of years. It wasn't much of a stretch to really imagine that magic was possible. Eric decided to just go with it.

"Yes…it. Is. Wednesday."

"Good," the owl replied, walking round Eric on legs made from thick twigs. Eric felt that he was being examined like a turkey at Christmas. The owl finished by leaping on to Eric's shoulder. It was as though a sack of potatoes had been dropped on him.

Eric managed to stay standing, if leaning a bit. There was a strong smell of the forest, a mix of stone, moss, cobwebs, and, of course, wood. Lots of different types of wood. Beech, elm, oak. He didn't realise how good his sense of smell was.

Toad introduced Eric, who felt the talons of the twig legs dig into his shoulder. There was a lot of strength in twigs, it appeared.

"Er-ric," the owl whispered close to Eric's ear. There was now the smell of pine. And something else. If he had to describe it, he would say it was the smell of *legends*. "Nope, not heard that name before, the owl continued, not letting go of Eric. Eric could smell more now – Time. *Future. Destiny? Hang on – how can you smell Destiny?*

The owl jumped and landed next to the cowering Toad and made a noise. Eric couldn't decide whether it was a *Brumph* or a repeat of *Hummpth*; however, it definitely wasn't a *Grufft*. Eric realised that analysing the mumblings of a magical owl wasn't going to help…

Eight

"Alan…big, fluffy cat," the owl said, facing the cat, who was now embarrassed. It seemed that the owl was trying to remember something. "Very big kitten," it added, "loves cuddles." Eric wasn't sure that you could *feel* someone grinning but he was positive that Toad was doing it right then. Alan's mouth formed a thin line.

"Of course," Alan muttered through gritted teeth, "we could go somewhere else for help?" Eric then noticed something out of the corner of his eye. *Did that tree just sneak away?*

Spude was his name. Well, technically, his name was Spudeferious the Wise, Master of Knowledge and Watcher of the Trees. He was also the owner of a vast collection of garden gnomes. But nobody mentioned that. Although everyone needs a hobby.

Spude (plus endless titles – see above) was what you would call a 'Spirit of the Forest'. He wasn't a natural owl, hadn't been for a very long time. An encounter with an evil badger over three hundred years ago had left Spude with no body. He was an essence, a 'thing' floating through time. After a hundred years he had got bored and managed to make himself a new body from what he could find in the woods. Things would have been different if he'd done it now. Spude's body would have been an old Cola can and his wings would have been made of plastic forks. During the Second World War Spude had experimented with using an old artillery shell he found when flying over the fields nearby. It didn't work well as a body. There was a big hole in one end and every time he flew the wind travelling through it created a such a noise that the people in the local area thought they were being bombed by another air raid. One old man took a shot at Spude with an ancient blunderbuss thinking he was the start of the invasion.

"Eric," Spude said again, the memory of small metal balls clattering noisily off his borrowed body appearing from nowhere. "*Hmm.*" He had to admit it though, this boy had a certain sense of stability about him. This was good. Spude was used to dealing with, for want of a better word, 'idiots'.

Alan had an amazingly daft ability to get angry (usually to do with Toad) and Toad, well, was like the annoying younger brother who thinks they are really funny but only knows two jokes and had told them seventeen times already. Maybe this boy would balance the other two out, make things *equal.* Spude liked equal.

The rain came to a stop. There was the sound of a million drops falling very slowly now from leaves and branches. Spude liked the drip-drip-drip-dry ability of wood. It meant he didn't have to use heat to dry off. If he ever caught fire, Spude decided that it would indeed look fantastic, unforgettable, awe-inspiring and, importantly, not last very long. An owl (any creature really) made out of dry wood has about as much chance of surviving a fire as a fish made from sherbet has of climbing out of a puddle it has just bravely dived into.

42

"Go on," Spude encouragingly said to Toad, "tell me. Everything." 'Everything' was said quite slowly.

So Toad told him all about Shadow, the missing children, breaking the silence between animals and humans and, of course, about Alan doing a wee on Toad to 'protect' him (Toad glared at Alan as he reported this bit). Eric wasn't sure if a wooden owl could actually smile, but he was pretty certain that a look of amusement crossed Spude's barky features – only for a moment though.

After the tale had been told to the owl, Spude stood deep in thought. Eric almost believed that the wooden bird had become a solid, carved statue again. So still and 'unalive'. Eric wanted to reach out just to stroke the detailed features before him; he realised that his hand was lifting to do just that and stopped himself.

"This. Cannot. Be," the owl uttered, growling low. Spude crouched on creaking legs and launched himself into the air, a faint trickles of sawdust and moss whirling behind him as he rose.

"It is all true, I tell you," Alan said, watching the owl circle overhead. "I swear by my tenth life." Eric had to think for a minute before he worked out what Alan had said. *Tenth life?* There was an old wives' tale about cats having nine lives, but this was silly. Or, thought Eric, after the rest of the evening's events this shouldn't surprise him. But he had to ask.

"Tenth life?"

"This is serious," Toad replied with a worried expression on his wide features. "Alan's just offered his last life for the truth!"

"What? I thought cats, I mean, people say that cats have

only nine lives!" Then Eric remembered that he was meant to be sensible. "Although, of course, they should have *only one*!"

"Alan has burned through his lives over the years…always offering himself to protect others." This actually worried Eric a little bit. He had had no idea about any of this, but certainly didn't want to imagine Alan dying for him!

The thoughts rattling around Eric's head were interrupted by Spude landing (crashing really) into a puddle, suddenly, causing a small tidal wave to erupt and more tiny woodland life to become the owners of flooded homes. The owl stared at Eric. Eric stared back. He felt that he was doing a lot of staring recently and wondered if someone could in fact make themselves ill by staring too much.

Eric tried not to look at Spude's beak, which had a drop of water hanging off it and was ready to fall at any moment. It was distracting; the protection of the local children and possibly saving the world was being put to the back of Eric's mind by a small drop of rainfall teetering on the beak of a wooden owl…

Nine

At school, Eric sat at his desk and thought about his new world. All morning. It was only at lunch time that he noticed there were a few less children in class.

"Where's Katie?" Eric asked Robin, who was engaged in investigating the inside of his right nostril with his finger.

"Dunno," came the reply, followed by a shrug of the shoulders. "Solomon isn't in either." That meant eight children from the village weren't in school. *Missing? Maybe. Worrying?* Yep. Eric thought that if this had been a film, some secret undercover government agents (with sunglasses) would have been sent to investigate (and would still wear the sunglasses inside). But no. There was just Eric. And a talking toad. And cat. And a strange owl 'thing'.

Shane still smiled a lot. This made all the other children unhappy as they didn't like it at all. *How could be so happy when so many of them were missing?*

Later that night, Eric wasn't surprised to find Spude in his bedroom along with Toad and Alan. His mother had just spoken to him about the amount of tea he had been drinking in his bedroom recently (and what was that dark stain on his bedroom carpet?) as he noticed a stack of used tea bags under his bed. And two dirty teacups. He looked at Toad. Toad shrugged, as if to say 'well, I like drinking tea'. Eric felt that he wouldn't get anywhere by arguing with Toad so decided to forget it for now and tell his mother in the morning that he had developed a taste for Earl Grey tea.

Eric's attention was drawn to a big pile of scrolls and books that had been dumped on his bed. They smelled old and were very, very dusty. It looked as though no one had read them for a long time. He wondered how they had been moved here with all the rain fall outside and how they could be so dry, then put that thought to the side. Distractions.

Toad jumped onto Eric's bed, causing a cloud of dust to puff upwards and give Eric a mild coughing fit. After a minute, Eric glared at Toad. He was still coughing and so did not think about the drink passed to him by Toad. Eric drank it to help the cough. Cold. Tea. *Ueergh.*

"Don't. Do. That. Again." He grated at the shamefaced amphibian. Eric then looked at the mountain of knowledge on his bed (through the still settling dust), resigned to the fact that he would have to change his duvet cover and bedsheets later.

He picked up a scroll at random and glanced at the drawings. There was a square in the middle with a further smaller square drawn within that. It could possibly, if you looked at it a certain way, resemble a door. Possibly. Around the outer square were crosses (or x's) spaced evenly apart drawn in a way that together made them look like a rough circle. There were nine crosses it total. Interesting.

"How do we get through all of this?" Eric asked, kneeling beside his bed and putting the scroll back on the pile. "I mean, I'm probably not going to understand a lot of it. What is it all?"

He grabbed an aged book with yellowed pages. He winced as a 'crack' sounded by the spine of the book resisting him opening it. Eric leafed through the book gently, slightly worried that he may damage it. Stopping at one page he pointed at the words scrawled in a spidery writing there. They were in a language that Eric didn't understand (but he knew it wasn't Welsh) and looked as though it had been written by someone who believed that all letters should be a triangle. He thrust the page at the owl. Spude looked at the mystical symbols and thought for a moment.

"That," the owl said after a minute, "is a recipe for leek and potato soup."

At dinner time, Eric's mother wasn't her usual chatty self. Eric asked her what was wrong.

"Oh, nothing, darling, nothing." She shook her head and smiled at Eric, although he noticed that she glanced at Eric's father as they all tucked into their food.

The bedroom was quiet. The bed had been cleaned, and new sheets plus duvet covers put on (which had taken some explanation by Eric to his parents involving him creating a story about 'allergies').

Eric lay in bed, feeling the softness of the new duvet and smelling the freshness of the sheets (he suspected it was that new washing powder of his mother's called 'Frush!', although any product that had an exclamation mark at the end was, Eric decided, a bit silly).

Eric realised that he had got used to the animals being around, and suddenly they were not there. Spude had gone back into the trees to find something (no idea what). Alan was out on patrol and who knew where Toad had got to. Eric also admitted that he probably wasn't going to get much sleep that night.

Even though his curtains were drawn, a shaft of moonlight invaded the small gap in the fabric. The pale beam of light came to rest on a small dark stain on the carpet. It was where Toad had first 'landed' in Eric's bedroom (and his life). Eric had tried to get the stain out; he was quite proud of himself, as it had been much worse before.

Frustrated at not being able to sleep, Eric threw back the bed covers and got out of his bed. He felt something soft and slightly (worryingly) moist under his foot. Looking down, he found that he was standing on a half-eaten cheese sandwich. With a used tea bag on top of it. Another reminder of Toad.

Eric stretched and walked over to the windows, peeking through the crack in the curtains. He had made sure that he had left enough of a gap when he opened the window earlier so that Alan (and Toad) could get back in.

He looked out into the dark garden. In the moonlight everything was painted shades of grey; and in some cases, just black. The lawn was, well, grey, the bushes dark grey, and the Eric gasped, as *something* ran across the lawn. It was a cat. He knew it wasn't Alan, as that particular feline would have shown up as light grey with slightly darker grey patches (white and ginger in night-time shades). The dark shape stopped. It turned a large head up towards Eric's window. Right at Eric. Pale green eyes stared up at Eric. They blinked. Once. Twice. Then they were gone.

Eric didn't realise that he had been holding his breath; he was rarely afraid of anything, but he had to admit to feeling slightly nervous now.

Ten

Eric backed away from the window, finally finding his bed again (and narrowly avoiding the already-mentioned cheese sandwich).

No, this wouldn't do at all! Eric decided that he would not just sit on his bed as though he were helpless and wait for things to happen. Not when he could do something (exactly what he could do, he wasn't sure just yet). Getting dressed quickly and quietly, Eric then eased open his bedroom door –which at that exact moment decided to develop a creaking hinge that it had never had before. Eric gritted his teeth and waited for his parents to appear with raised voices or questioning looks. Or both. Nothing. With a glare at the door that had betrayed him, Eric crept along the landing to the stairs.

As he got nearer the bottom, Eric heard voices coming from the living room. Mum and Dad. They sounded worried.

"It's not safe for him any more," Eric's father said, "I've said it so many times before, I can't count. We should have moved house years ago!" This was a surprise to Eric, who had been happy living in the village and had never thought that his parents had ever wanted to leave.

"I know you never liked living here near the graveyard," Eric's mother replied, "but this is Eric's house, remember? Your mum left it to him in her will." Another surprise. Will? What was that about his grandmother? And what was that about his own house? Why had he never been told about any of this?

Eric couldn't remember much about his grandmother. She had died when he was only two years old. He did have one or two memories of a mass of long flowing grey hair and eyes that sparkled like jewels next to a bonfire. (Eric was sure that this was indeed a good way to describe his grandmother's eyes and that she did, in fact, not have eyes that actually sparkled, as that would be silly. And quite dangerous. It just sounded good).

There was only one picture of her that Eric knew of, and that was a pencil drawing (a really, *really* good one, almost lifelike) hanging on the wall just above the row of pegs for coats next to the front door. Eric's mother said that the drawing was almost as good as a real photograph. Eric's father had told him that it had been drawn a couple of months before his grandmother had died.

Eric looked up at that picture now. His grandmother was there, her long hair cascading around her shoulders and a slight grin creasing her face. She wasn't looking straight out of the picture, but to the right, as though she was thinking something that had amused her. Eric felt a single tear escape his left eye and make its way slowly down his cheek. He turned back towards the living room.

Eric stopped his hand as he reached for the door handle. His father was still talking and Eric could only stand and listen.

"They were always hanging around here. All around the house. I asked her not to let them in, but did she listen?" Eric thought that his father had been drinking beer. "I never let them in, but sometimes I would come down in the morning and I knew they'd been here." There was a very long pause and a 'glugging' sound – definitely drinking beer. "Small crumbs in corners and under the bed; food going missing, then of course the paw prints." More glugging, along with a light 'slurp' which was probably Eric's mother drinking her wine from a glass. "Damn animals."

"You've always liked Alan, dear," Eric's mother said.

"Well," *glug*, "that's different, I mean," *glug*, "Alan's *our* cat, isn't he? Always has been, always will." *Glug*.

Eric didn't remember the animals. Well, except Alan. He'd always been there. He was sure that there had only ever been Alan. Alan was his cat, his pet, his friend. Alan had been there when Eric needed a cuddle to cheer up, someone to talk to (which Eric now realised had been a very strange situation as Alan would have been able to talk back at Eric at any time), and someone to just 'be there'.

Eric slowly crept backwards from the door and instead went into the kitchen to grab a biscuit; then, not looking back at the living room, he quietly put his coat on, opened the front door and went out into the night.

Even though it was late, dark and gloomy, Eric wasn't worried about going out. He didn't know where he was going, and if he was honest, he wasn't really caring at the moment where he ended up. The tears had stopped now, drying on his face and making his skin feel a bit tight in the cool night air.

There was a lot rattling around inside Eric's head. Grandmother. Alan. Missing children. His own house! Oh, and talking animals! A week ago the biggest problem Eric faced was making sure that no one put his books in the wrong order (always alphabetical, thank you).

Eric was so caught up in his thoughts that he nearly jumped out of his skin when a big black cat brushed up against his leg and slinked off. Calming down, Eric watched the cat go, before turning and continuing his walk.

He decided he would go and see Robin. The other boy lived only a ten minute walk from Eric and even though it was late Eric knew that his friend would be awake. Robin had told Eric a few years ago that he didn't sleep much. However, Robin hadn't mentioned exactly what he did instead. Eric assumed Robin practised picking his nose (as he seemed very good at it).

There was one major thing that was bothering Eric; Alan had been around for him when he needed him, and he was a pet. But Eric couldn't remember Alan ever being a kitten...

Eleven

Eric knew something was wrong when he saw the police car outside Robin's house. He crept round to the back of the house (he and Robin had done this many times before) and peeked in at the window to the living room.

Robin's mother (curly ginger hair, just like her son. Oh, and glasses too) was sitting on the sofa, her head in her hands. She was shaking. It took Eric a moment to realise that she was crying. No, not crying – sobbing. Sobbing as though her life were leaving her body. *What was going on?*

A male police officer with a serious but sympathetic face was sitting next to Robin's mother, holding out a tissue for her. They looked worried too. Robin's father was talking to another police officer (female) by the fireplace.

Usually so neat and tidy, Robin's father was a mess. His hair was plastered with sweat, the small bald patch glistening in the light cast from the living room table lamps. The shirt he was wearing was crumpled and his tie hung loosely around his neck.

Eric decided to take a further look. He and Robin had worked out a way of sneaking into Robin's house about a year ago; (They had been watching a television show about the history of England *that they probably shouldn't have been watching and their parents would be disappointed*; however, it had lots of battle scenes, that involved blood, heads flying off and torture. As such, it was on late at night and, luckily, Robin had a television in his bedroom). The plan involved climbing up a drainpipe and pushing part of the windowpane in so that he could get into Robin's bedroom (it wasn't a complicated operation). Luckily the drainpipe was right next to where Eric was crouching!

Eric put his foot on the massive bolts holding the drainpipe in place and started his climb. It was pretty easy work (he *had* done it one hundred and sixty-two times; Eric remembered statistics).

Climbing into Robin's bedroom, Eric had a quick look for any changes. There were none. It was still a shocking terrible mess. In fact, the pile of washing that Eric had sat on last time he was here (a week last Wednesday) was still there.

Creeping across the room, Eric resisted the urge to put the light on. He was sure that someone in the house would notice. If not Robin's parents, then definitely the police (they do things like that). So, a search in darkness was his only option. Getting closer to the door, Eric opened it very slowly (hoping that this door would not betray him like his bedroom door had done) so that he could hear what was going on downstairs.

It was all a jumble. Robin's mother was still wailing and crying; Robin's father was still talking. Eric couldn't make out what was being said. He knew that it was bad though. He realised that he wasn't going to find anything out this way. Shutting the door (very carefully), he took another look round the room before he went (in the dark, as noted earlier).

Robin's book collection was nothing at all like Eric's; Eric liked facts, whereas Robin enjoyed stories involving cars exploding and wizards turning people into cheese. Cheese with faces (Robin definitely had a book where that happened. The cheese also talked).

Just before he reached the window to make his escape, Eric brushed against a pile of comics in the darkness. Luckily, he managed to catch them before they fell and gave him away. However, one comic was thinner than the others. It was glossy, and smooth.

Eric realised that it was a plastic wallet, just like his teacher used at school. Without thinking, Eric took it to the open window so that the moonlight would show him what Robin had found so interesting.

It was a photograph, enlarged to fit the plastic wallet. Eric didn't see anything remarkable about it. There was a ruined building (burned down, Eric reckoned); the stone walls half collapsed and some wooden beams sticking out of the rubble like nails waiting to be hammered into a plank.

Why did Robin have this? Looking further, Eric noticed parts of furniture in the ruins; a wrecked bookcase, some chairs. And an old, weathered soot-stained writing desk. Eric couldn't be sure, but he thought that he could see a fire-blackened chain attached to the desk. This was all very, very strange. And very puzzling.

Even though he had no idea why, Eric decided that this was important. Did it have anything to with Robin? Did it have to do with why the police were here? It was obvious to Eric that Robin had gone missing. Just like the other children.

The house was dark when Eric got back home. He knew his parents would have gone to bed. Stopping briefly in the kitchen and quietly making himself a sandwich (tuna – there was no cheese left) Eric then crept upstairs to his bedroom. All was quiet.

Alan was fast asleep in the corner, the big cat's fur rising and falling in time with his breathing. Toad put a stubby foreleg to his mouth as if to say 'quiet' as Eric sat down next to him.

"Couldn't sleep," Eric explained before Toad asked. Toad nodded.

"I never really have trouble sleeping," Toad said, picking a crumb off his belly that had somehow appeared from nowhere. *Even when I was a prisoner, I just dropped off when it was time.* Eric thought for a moment.

"You never said where that was." Toad didn't reply. "It must have been nearby. To think that you'd been there all that time!"

Toad's reply was cut short by Alan jumping up and hissing.

"Shadow. He's here!"

Twelve

"I can smell him," Alan snapped, his nose wrinkled and twisted in an effort to find his foe.

"What? Where? How?" Toad rattled off the basic questions as he didn't know what to ask. Then he added, "Who?" to make sure he'd got them all. "Why?" He'd forgotten that one.

Alan was pacing round the room sticking his nose into corners, Eric's bed sheets and even (Eric winced at this) Eric's laundry basket.

"How do you know?" Eric asked, not really knowing what to do.

"His stink is all round here," Alan muttered, "all round…you." Eric stood still as Alan came closer, the cat's nose twitching quickly as he got nearer. Alan's eyes narrowed in anger. "He's on you!"

Toad, who had been climbing onto Eric's bed in search of a biscuit he had spotted before, suddenly shocked, forgot how to climb and landed on the bedroom carpet with a 'splat'.

"How has Shadow got near?" Toad asked, too confused to even get up off his back from where he had landed.

Eric, not used to the idea of not having a clue what was going on, stood there open mouthed. He shut it. He opened it again. Eric looked down to where Alan was nuzzling against his trouser leg.

"Got you!" Alan exclaimed. The cat used his claws like a pair of tweezers to pluck something off Eric's trousers. Cat, toad and boy all bent forward to examine the find.

"Well, just a cat hair?" Eric frowned, thinking about that black cat that had brushed up to him when he was out before. "Why is that important?"

Both Toad and Alan were speechless, and for once, there was a silent agreement between them. They looked at Eric as though he had asked the question 'what's the problem with shaving cats, painting them yellow and pretending they're just lions who are a bit unwell?'.

"What?" Eric was greeted with exactly the same expression as before (although if it was possible for a toad to have eyebrows, they would have been raised even higher for dramatic effect).

"This. Is. Shadow's. Hair!" Alan said slowly, shaking the offending item between his claws in the air above his head.

"How did Shadow's hair get on you?" Toad shook his head as he asked, all serious for once.

"Er…" Eric replied.

"Forget it. We need to protect the house and get a message to Spude!"

"Protect the house?" Eric was, again (and he was getting a bit fed up with it now), confused.

"I'll do protection," Alan said, turning to Toad. "You get word to Spude." Toad nodded and waddled off. Alan looked back at Eric. "We need eggs."

"Eggs?"

"Yep. Lots of 'em!"

"Normal eggs or free range? Or organic? Or are they

the same thing?"

"Let's just go to the kitchen."

Toad realised shortly after he had left that he should have let Alan do the 'message' thing and then he could have stayed inside to do the 'protect house duty'. After over a hundred years of doing very little physical activity, Toad wished he had eaten less cheese sandwiches at Eric's and drank water instead of tea (with three sugars in).

Still, he was making progress (he had left the garden, stopped for ten minutes to get his breath back ad wheezed his way past the treeline and into the woods). As he went along however, Toad began to feel that he was being watched. (There's always someone watching you in a wood. It's an unwritten rule). The problem was, Toad couldn't be sure. It was as though there was something to the left *and* the right, watching his waddling tubbiness amble along.

Toad also realised that looking for Spude was not one of the easiest things he could be doing. You didn't find Spude, he appeared out of a tree. As he was in a wood surrounded by trees, Toad knew that Spude's 'appearance' could come from anywhere. At any time. Which was a bit worrying. It was going to take some luck for Toad to find Spude.

Then, Toad saw something (well, two things, really) that gave him an idea…

The door to his parents' room was shut. Eric knew that both his mother and father were heavy sleepers; even so, he was cautious as he reached the bottom of the stairs and followed Alan into the kitchen.

"Shall I put the light on?" whispered Eric.

"Can do. We won't wake anyone." Eric didn't ask a question. Alan just looked at Eric's face. "It's a cat thing," Alan explained, "don't ask me how or why. Cats have always been able to send people to sleep." Eric sat down at the kitchen table. Alan stopped inspecting the eggs on top of the fridge and jumped onto the table in front of Eric.

"You know how there are times that when a cat curls up next to you, purrs and makes you feel safe and warm?" Eric nodded. "Over a thousand years ago my ancestors realised that this ability can send humans into a deep slumber."

"Really? Were there any tests done? Any facts?" Alan wrinkled his face as he thought about this.

"He was called Dave?"

"Anyway…" Eric wished he'd never asked. "Why do we need eggs?"

"Well, have we got any grenades?"

"No."

"Throwing knives?"

"No."

"Then we'll be using eggs."

Thirteen

Howard and Balthazar were snails. There was nothing special about them. They were snails. They were known for miles around for, well, nothing.

Technically, this wasn't true. They'd known about *everything* all along and there were rumours that they'd planned it all (when we say that, we mean the mysteries of the universe, such as why one sock disappears in a washing machine). No one suspects snails. No one thinks that snails have any secrets. The snails Howard and Balthazar had plans for it ALL. Only a handful of animals (certainly not people) knew about the snails and their powers.

If you said that snails were slow, boring, not very interesting and pointless then a lot of others in the world would agree with you. However, if you said that snails were in fact highly intelligent geniuses with dreams of world conquest, magical abilities and had the type of personality that you would find in a super villain, then you would be laughed at. A lot. Those who were laughed at ended up disappearing in odd circumstances.

The two snails were busy minding their own business (they didn't look busy – they were snails). Howard gave Balthazar a quick look as a waddling shape loomed through the trees towards them. Balthazar nodded his eye stalks a little. He too has seen Toad appear. A passing squirrel would later tell his squirrel friends that he had seen two snails sighing in frustration. No one believed him. The squirrel was laughed at. He disappeared two days later.

Out of breath, Toad skidded to a halt in front of the snails. They didn't blink or move, instead doing a perfect impersonation of 'snails'.

"Sorry to bother you," Toad started, realising that he wouldn't get much back in the way conversation, "but have you seen Spude?"

Eric wasn't sure what he was meant to be looking for. If he was honest with himself, he didn't really know exactly what was going on. All he knew was that Alan was nervously glaring out of the kitchen window then examining the row of eggs on the table.

"Do we need to boil them or anything?" Eric asked, watching uselessly as Alan gently poked and prodded each egg. The cat raised his eyebrows and looked at Eric.

"Never thought about it," Alan mumbled, "but it'll just waste time anyway."

"Do we need to paint them green to look like grenades?"

Alan stood on all four paws and looked directly at Eric with a hard stare.

"It's not about the… colour. It's about what they do."

"They…explode?" Alan closed his eyes and thought for a moment.

"Eggs are the best way of fighting things in the darkness."

"You do realise what you've just said, don't you?"

"Yes."

"Only the same effect can be gained by turning the

lights on." Alan sighed very heavily, taking his time to reply.

"When I say *darkness*, I mean evil. Nasty things. Creatures that…" A sound like knives clattering over roof tiles cut Alan short. "Outside!" Eric rushed to the window, trying to get a glimpse of whatever was making that awful noise. Alan jumped up onto the windowsill next to Eric, frantically scanning the darkness of the garden.

"Get. An. Egg," Alan ordered.

Eric grabbed one of the 'grenades' off the table and handed it to Alan. Alan looked at it. "Don't give it to me!" The cat snapped, opening the window as wide as his furry paws could. "Throw it out there!"

Eric did as he was told. Both cat and boy heard the *splatchruccch* that perfectly describes the sound of an egg breaking. The other noise stopped, followed by a slight hiss like a snake with a blocked nose. Nothing else happened. Nothing moved.

After a minute Alan gestured outside.

"Let's have look," he said, not bothering to use the cat flap in the kitchen door but simply jumping lightly out of the window he'd opened. Eric did the same, instead of going to the door and opening it like a human (he thought it would save time).

They were able to use the light cast through the kitchen window to locate the smashed egg. Now, Eric had seen many smashed eggs in his short life (and had caused quite a few during cooking classes at school) and he didn't think that any would be special. However, what he saw on the ground in the dim light from the house was like nothing he had EVER seen before.

And again – Now, Eric had seen many foot / paw / claw prints in his short life (but hadn't caused any when cooking at school – although Robin had when he'd stepped in some split flour) and he didn't think any would be special. However, this was astonishing.

As Alan nosed around the remains of the smashed egg, Eric couldn't believe what he was seeing. He knew that an egg didn't cause much of a 'spread' with what was inside it when smashed but the yolk was covering nearly three feet of garden in a very rough circular patch.

The first stir of fear crept into Eric's heart as he looked at the *other* feature of the mess.

It was a large, blackened footprint.

It was too big to be a cat. Or a dog. Or a big dog. Or a bigger dog. Or a monstrous demon dog that eats horses. And it wasn't just the size – Eric was sure that the print had been made by a *skeleton* of an animal.

"Don't worry, it won't come back for a while," Alan said, prodding the egg with a claw, "this will have scared it off." Eric had one or two questions (which he thought was surprising, as surely this situation would have rated at least five or six questions, especially involving the word 'What?').

"Why won't it come back?" Eric asked, surprised at how calm he was, "and what was it?"

"Well, there isn't a short answer..." Alan cleared his throat for a long chat.

Fourteen

"Dragons don't exist." Eric couldn't believe what he was hearing. Then he thought for a moment. In the past few days he had found out that animals could talk, use magic and have been fighting each other for hundreds of years. Maybe dragons were not so silly an idea as Eric thought. Well, crocodiles were a sort of dragon, weren't they?

"Think of all the creatures that you've been told don't exist," Alan said as Eric had no choice but to listen. "We've covered dragons. But there's more." The cat hesitated as he thought about how he was going to explain this. He gave up. "Look, you must have a book on myths and legends that you've read? You're a boy!"

Both the cat and Eric were alerted by the sounds of grunting behind them. They turned to see Toad struggling with a large book, dragging it across the floor. He stopped, flopping down on top of it, out of breath.

"I think I'm dead!" Toad gasped between taking in great gulps of air. "I'm a thinker, not a dragger." Eric picked up the book and looked at the cover.

"Legends of Bygone Days?" He frowned. "This isn't mine. I don't have books like this."

Toad shook his warty head. "Nope," (gasp) "I," (gasp) "found it!" (gasp) "In your" (gasp) "dad's room" (final gasp and collapse into silence).

Alan explained as much as he could whilst Toad slept (although Eric suspected that Toad had actually fainted because he was, well, a toad not used to exercise and was deeply unfit).

Eric ran everything back through his mind – Mythical beasts used to not only exist, but ran free all over Great Britain. Dragons, Griffons, Unicorns, Werewolves (Eric did struggle believing that last one), Imps and Demons. Eric's logical brain accepted a lot of this after some thought. Beasts were Beasts, weren't they? Things evolve over time, others die out?

It was the egg explanation that really confused Eric though.

According to Alan, a lot of the animals of myth were good, noble creatures. Even the werewolves. Most were destroyed several hundred years ago (in a weird spell disaster that Alan couldn't explain properly). Many were buried in special places and time took its toll on the remains. However, sometimes the bones survive.

"And the bones are what Shadow is after," Alan whispered. Eric just looked at the cat, knowing that Alan would continue. "All of those creatures are gone. But," Alan swallowed, "if the bones exist then some kind of 'ghost' can be brought back and attached to the bones." Alan tried to ignore the look in Eric's eyes and continued. "Just the bones though. The magic involved is dark, impure and evil. This has an effect on the bones…it…twists the spirit of the creature that was. The bone ghost becomes a being of darkness itself. Bad magic creates bad effects."

Eric nodded. This did make more sense than he felt it had any right to. He waved a hand for Alan to say more.

"What I'm saying is, if you want to bring a dead dragon or whatever back, then you can. But it'll be just the bones and a bad attitude."

Things clicked together in Eric's head.

"Shadow wants a load of long dead creatures just as evil as him?" Alan nodded.

"He'll take any he can get. But it's the dragons. It's the dragons he wants above all others."

"Why?"

"They're big, scary, bad tempered and will be under his control." Alan then added, "This should be self-explanatory."

"But the eggs?"

Alan blinked a few times.

"Ah, the eggs. Well, any eggs would do."

"What, even frogspawn?"

"In…theory, I suppose."

"Right."

"Eggs are a symbol of new life. Purity. There's no evil in an egg. It's innocent. Bad things can't cope with eggs."

Eric slapped the kitchen table in understanding.

"And that's why whatever was outside disappeared!" He thought then said, "Why was it all black?"

"You're catching on to this. The pure nature of the egg, well, more or less *burns* those creatures that have been raised from the dead."

"So…like vampires and holy water, in those stupid films?"

Alan narrowed his eyes.

"Don't get me started on vampires…we'll talk about those later…"

Outside, Eric looked again at the modern artwork entitled 'Smashed Egg Dead Creature Footprint'. In a weird way, he supposed, this made sense. The monstrous footprint did indeed appear to be burnt. The bright orange-yellow of the egg was mixed with the black shape of the print.

Standing up, Eric went back inside to where Toad and Alan were talking. Something had been bothering Eric, like a fly bussing against a closed window. Now he realised what it was.

"This is why children are going missing, isn't it?" he asked, sitting down at the table. Toad finally nodded.

"Yes. It's all part of Shadow's plan."

"But why has he not tried to take me?" There was a look between the cat and the toad.

"You know that book on legends and myths we looked at before?" When Eric nodded, Toad continued, "Well, did you happen to notice who wrote it?"

Fifteen

Eric fetched the book, shaking his head as he went. What else was going to happen? He'd learned that the house he lived in was actually his and that animals had always been around his family.

Picking up the book, Eric glanced at the name on the spine. He had to read it again. And again. Slowly, he walked back to the kitchen and placed the book carefully in front of Toad and Alan. Eric looked at the book then at the animals.

"What's going on with this?" Eric asked them, his voice a croaking whisper. All three of them looked at the book again and at the name of the author that was stamped on the spine in faded silver and blue letters.

Marjorie Cerridwen.

Eric's Grandmother…

Eric didn't manage to speak to his parents before he went to school the next day. He really wanted to, just to find out what was going on with the house and his grandmother. However, he was also just a little bit angry that they had kept something as important as this from him.

School started off in as another boring day but swiftly became if not better, then much more dramatic (and scary). They had PE that morning and Eric couldn't stop looking around the changing room and thinking about how there were fewer kitbags and clothes than there had been just a month ago.

Walking past the lockers, Eric's eye was drawn to the colour red. Well, not red, exactly, more…reddish, like hair.

Just like Robin's hair.

Looking closer, Eric found tufts of curly reddish hair sticking in the door of one of the lockers. As everyone else went outside, Eric asked permission to go to the toilet, then left the changing rooms and walked the short journey down corridor to the toilet. He waited five minutes then went back.

Eric pushed the door of the changing rooms open, walking in and quickly looking round. He knew something was wrong, but…what? Eric sat on the bench underneath his clothes' peg to think. He could hear the other children outside shouting in excitement as the PE lesson carried on, only broken by the sharp shriek of the teacher's whistle in the background.

In the changing room, all was silent…

Except it wasn't. Eric was sure that he could detect the sound of breathing; slow and fain, right…behind him! Eric snapped his head round and peeked through the clothes hanging from his peg.

Over in the corner, just out of sight from the door, was Robin. Only he was lying there, staring and the ceiling and not moving apart from the breathing that Eric had just heard. As he watched, a big black cat stalked out from behind a locker and climbed slowly onto Robin's chest. The cat stood there as Robin's chest went up and down, looking intently at the still face and staring eyes of the unmoving boy.

Eric knew that he should do something; but he

was…scared. He wasn't used to this, being scared was something new. All he could do was watch.

The cat purred to itself happily and lowered its head so that its eyes directly in front of Robin's. The cat's mouth opened and the purring slowly changed into words, strange words that Eric could not understand.

Eric was stuck staring as the cat's words got louder and louder. Robin's body began shaking, making the cat tremble as it fought to keep its balance on Robin's chest. Eric opened his mouth to scream but nothing came out. There were no other sounds, no shouting from outside, not even a shrill whistle. There were only the words. Eric knew he needed Toad. And Alan. But he was on his own.

Suddenly the words stopped. The cat rose up as though it had been struck and fell off Robin's now unmoving chest. It curled into a ball lay still. Eric crept out from his hiding place and cautiously edged closer to the cat.

It was bigger than Eric thought. Even though it wasn't moving, it still made Eric feel wary. The cat's eyes were wide open, two green marbles staring at the wall as its mouth formed an unmoving snarl. As he looked closer, Eric noticed that the cat was missing half of its left ear, as though it had been ripped off in a fight.

Eric was about to check on Robin when the cat's chest heaved and it made a screeching that pricked at the inside of Eric's ears. Eric ducked back behind his hanging clothes and watched in horror as the next minute of his life became the scariest he'd ever had.

As Eric watched, the cat grew in length as its fur shrank back inside its skin! The ears shrivelled back to the sides of the head and the whiskers fell out onto the tiled floor of the changing room.

Mouth open, the cat's teeth morphed so that they became flatter and the jaw widened to allow the teeth room. Eric held his breath as the paws became hands and feet; the long black tail shortened and eventually disappeared.

But the eyes didn't change.

As the fur on the creature's head became straggly hair Eric was horrified to see that he was looking at Shane!

Eric could do nothing but watch as Shane left Robin's still form and ripped open a locker (and the fact that Shane was naked didn't help Eric's feelings of horror).

It was the same locker door that Eric had seen the reddish tufts of hair sticking out of.

Shane then turned and grabbed Robin's feet, dragging the boy into the locker. Then, crouching down, Shane stuck his head out of the locker, took hold of the door, and slammed it behind him. And Robin was gone!

Sixteen

The 'clang' of the locker door slamming closed rattled around Eric's head the rest of the day. He didn't tell anyone about what he's seen. He couldn't. Eric had no idea who he could tell, and who would actually believe him (apart from some talking animals, which is, you will admit, stretching people's belief).

Eric didn't know how he walked home that day. He didn't pay any attention to anything. When his parents said hello to him Eric just gave a mumbled 'meh' in reply and 'cup of tea please'. He knew Toad and Alan would be waiting for him.

Alan sighed, looking at Eric with deep sorrowful eyes.

"Shadow was always able to change his shape," he said slowly, "it's one of his...gifts."

"At least I know why Shane was so good at climbing," Eric muttered.

"And he was always better at magic than me," added Alan. Eric noticed that Toad nodded. The boy frowned.

"Is there anything else you're not telling me?" he asked.

"Shadow and Alan have been fighting for a very long time," Toad explained, "you remember Shadow's ear?" Eric thought about the torn ear of the cat and nodded. "Well...Alan did that."

"Good," Eric said, and meant it. He didn't like the cat

who had taken his friends. "It makes sense, especially if they were enemies."

There was a look between Alan and Toad that Eric found suspicious.

"We weren't very old…and I was careless," Alan began, lost in a sea of memories, "we were only playing." Alan didn't like thinking about the times when they were innocent. When they were just kittens.

"Shadow lost a lot of blood and nearly died," Toad continued for Alan, "and Spude couldn't do anything. If your grandmother hadn't helped them…" Toad's voice trailed off as he realised that he had said much more than he had intended to.

Eric leaned forward, frowning.

"Tell. Me. Now."

Spude flew to the graveyard as quickly as he could. He hadn't been here for a very long time. There was something he had to do, something that would take a lot of focus and energy.

Flying out of the trees he found the grave he was looking for and landed on the headstone. Spude felt a moment of sadness as his gaze crossed the name of who was buried beneath the earth there.

'MARJORIE CERRIDWEN'

Eric needed time to take in this new information. Alan and Shadow were hundreds of years old and yet his grandmother had saved Shadow when he was only a kitten?

Eric remembered his grandmother dying, but she had not been over eighty years old (seventy-nine to be exact, so nearly). Definitely not nearly the nine hundred that Toad and Alan claimed…

Speaking to Eric's grandmother would drain Spude massively, but it had to be done. Spude was ancient, had vast amounts of knowledge and could work out problems that would make the argument about *where life started* been like two plus two. But Mother Cerridwen was something else. Wise beyond belief.

Spude gripped the top of the headstone with his twig legs and closed his eyes. The creak of his wooden body in the faint breeze was the only sound in the graveyard (even the local hedgehog who never stopped singing wasn't around – he was currently lost in the next village looking for a squirrel who had told him about intelligent snails). The wind picked up. Spude could feel the headstone trembling under his feet.

His eyes snapped open as the power of the oldest witch in England hit him, even from beyond the grave. Spude spoke words from his beak that did not come from inside him, but somewhere old and dark-

Protect my Grandson…

Shadow had a thought. It was an evil thought. It was possibly the evillest, nastiest though that he had ever had. It gave birth to an idea, and that idea became a plan.

Shadow knew exactly how he could stop that boy interfering in his plans and also take his enemies down at the same time. The black cat allowed himself a wicked grin. This would serve everyone right. Alan and Toad and that ridiculous wooden owl.

Shadow started laughing…

Seventeen

"She wasn't really old." Toad was trying to explain. "Your granny always seemed to know when we needed help and she would be there. Sometimes she was young, and sometimes she was older. But that first time, when Shadow needed saving, she was older than we'd ever see her."

"So, Granny saved Shadow hundreds of years ago when she was and old woman?" Eric was still struggling with this.

"There isn't an easy way of explaining this," Alan said, "Spude had an idea some time ago that Grandmother Cerridwen could, well, travel to where she was needed." Alan touched the scar between his eyes; Eric never knew what had caused it. "Your Gran healed me here," Alan continued, "but she… was younger then."

"Was this after she saved Shadow?"

"Some years later," Alan replied, "Shadow gave me this when we fought over the Vole Kingdom."

"What's the Vole Kingdom?"

"Forget about that for now." Toad climbed into Eric's lap and looked at him with an expression of worry.

Eric didn't know why but he had a sudden urge to stroke the top of Toad's rough head. He stopped himself before he came into contact with the warty skin.

Something had kicked a memory (or two) into his mind. Eric's grandmother had gone away now and then; but was always home the next day. But she couldn't have, could she? Time Travel? Eric had to admit that this was a bit beyond his big collection of *facts* that he had in his head and in his big collection of books.

All three (boy, toad and cat) jumped as there was a clattering at the window. They turned to the sound, a sound like wooden beads being thrown at glass.

It made sense when they saw that it was Spude knocking at the window with his wood-based body parts. Eric hoped his parents hadn't heard the knocking. Opening the window Eric was then used as a handy perch for the owl who landed on Eric's shoulder.

"Fire!" Spude said quietly. "Fire!" Eric glanced round, seeing no flames or smoke. He raised an eyebrow as he looked back at the owl.

"Follow the fire," Spude went on, "that's what she said!"

"Who?" he asked, although he was starting to suspect something and was going to have strong words with a few people, especially his parents if they everyone survived the next few days.

"Follow...the...fire..." Spude whispered before falling silent.

"Oh." Eric rubbed his eyes in frustration. "Fire."

The other looked at him with questioning looks. He shook his head.

"Fire. I'm and idiot..."

Spude had known something (but there was nothing new there – he always did). Why had the owl perched on the Cerridwen hag's grave like that? Shadow couldn't work that out. Spude hadn't seen the dark form of Shadow watching him from the trees.

For a brief moment, the horrible flicker or concern caught hold of the evil cat's heart – would that ridiculous owl be able to hamper Shadow's plan? Especially the new part of the plan?

Should he care? He was close, very close. His preparations were nearly complete. Shadow just wondered who else he would have to kill at some point for the simple fact of *getting in the way.*

Pale green eyes blinked once before the shape of a big black cat walked out of the trees from where it had been hidden.

And into the graveyard...

"Here" Eric tossed the photograph of the ruined building he'd found in Robin's bedroom on the kitchen table. He pointed to the scorch marks and soot. "Fire. We have to follow it." Eric remembered that Robin liked taking photographs and so hadn't thought about a random snap like this appearing in the boy's room.

Toad's mouth fell open as he looked at the image. "No...he couldn't have...I was kept there for years!" Toad started to shake with anger. Or shame. Maybe both. "How did I not see this?" Toad shouted, jumping off the table.

"What, that old cottage? Alan was confused. "You were there? For all that time?" The cat laughed. "I don't know if that's funny or tragic."

"You really had no idea Toad was being kept there?" Eric asked. Then he thought. "Hang on – where is this?"

"Another of Shadow's talents – he can hide things," Toad muttered, "but where did this come from?"

"I found it in Robin's bedroom."

Everyone was now confused.

"Did Robin ever do anything or say anything odd?" Alan asked. Eric had long think about this; there were too many events to even begin creating a list of odd things that Robin had done. Such as the time when he tried to steal a penguin from the zoo using a balloon and a shoebox (Eric could never figure out the reason for the balloon). There had been another time when Robin had said that he could walk through walls, but only if he closed his eyes. He hadn't been in hospital very long afterwards however. Eric had been the one who phoned for the ambulance.

"His mum was always telling him off for doing silly things," Eric said, "like blowing his nose on his sleeve, eating his earwax, leaving cat hairs on the sofa when…they…didn't…have…a …cat?"

Everyone looked at each other.

"Shadow has been using Robin as his eyes and ears in the school." Spude realised.

"We have to go and look at this," Alan decided, pointing at the photograph. More nodding from all.

"Bring the rest of those eggs," Toad added as they all went to the door.

Eighteen

Eric couldn't believe that he had never noticed the cottage before. It was there right in front of him. Well, it was a burned ruin now, but it was still there regardless. Alan and Toad were poking around in the ash, dirt and wood whilst Spude perched on a roof beam that had been lucky enough to escape the fire (and was now in danger of rotting due to exposure to too much rain).

"Here," Toad nudged the scorched desk in front of him, "this is where I was kept." Eric carefully picked his way through the wreckage to stand next to Toad. He looked from the desk to the chain that he assumed was the one that had held Toad. Toad sighed. "I found out what Shadow was up to, but I didn't know he'd focus his power here."

"So what you're saying is," Eric said, scratching his nose in thought, "that Shadow was able to stop everyone from seeing this cottage? In a clearing in a wood near a small town?"

"It doesn't matter now," Alan grumbled, picking bits of ash out of his fur, "now we're here, let's figure out what we need to do."

Follow The Fire. That's what Spude had been told. Eric wondered how the fire had started (he'd assumed Toad was responsible somehow).

"I don't know," replied Toad when Eric asked him. "I managed to get out, then the cottage sort of…well…blew up?" Toad noticed the looks his friends were giving him. "I didn't start it."

"Let's look over there," Eric said, pointing to a patch of scorched wood that seemed to be a lot blacker than the other burned areas. "It looks like it used to be a chair," he said, nudging a longer piece of charred wood with his foot. "This was probably one of the legs."

Toad plopped himself down next to the blackened collection of wood and peered at it. "Shadow kept a wooden box on this chair," Toad said, "there was something in it that held power." He hesitated before adding, "A lot of power. I'm sure it was something he was using to help him hide this place." Eric noticed that his companions looked serious.

"Shadow is an exceptionally powerful magic user," Spude said, an edge of worry creeping into his voice. "So if he needed to use the power of something else to help him, then that spell would be big. Very big."

"So, whatever caused the fire started here?" Eric wondered, scanning the rest of the wreckage. "*Hmm.* But I still don't understand. Follow The Fire. What does it tell us?"

Spude looked at Toad. "How big was that box Shadow had?"

Toad used his stubby arms to full extent to show Spude a decent guess at the size.

"And what was it made of?" Spude was starting to suspect that the magic Shadow had been using was way more powerful than they had thought.

"I dunno," Toad replied, "it was dark. Never really seen wood like it."

"Dark?"

"Yeah, almost black."

"That doesn't sound odd," Eric commented, "Ebony is very dark and there are other types of wood as well." Spude bowed his head and closed his eyes.

"Not like this," Spude whispered after a minute of thought. "If this wood is what I think it is then it has power in itself. I didn't know there was any left. The last I heard about it was a couple of hundred years ago."

Eric noticed the worried look that appeared on the faces of Alan and Toad.

"What?"

"Schwarzwald," Alan answered. The cat seemed, to Eric, almost afraid to say the word. "It only grows in a small number of places."

"Never ever heard of that," Eric commented.

"It only grows where the bodies of dragons lie," Spude said solemnly. "Myths claim that the trees that grow around dragon graves absorb the magic and essence of the dead and it becomes almost black with power."

"Only dark and evil things come after something has died, Eric. Remember?" Toad asked Eric, who nodded. "So, this dark wood infused with dark magic can be used to contain good magic."

"And use it to make dark magic stronger?" Eric finished. He'd managed to figure this out and, even though things seemed really bad at the moment, he was still quite pleased with himself.

"Correct," Spude answered.

Eric was about to sit on a pile of charred wood when a thought struck him.

"You said there was no more of this wood anywhere…" Eric then realised that he should have sat down for this, "so you're saying that Shadow has found some?" Eric finally gave up and sat down. "That means he was able to find the grave of a dragon!"

Scratching at the hag's grave with a claw, Shadow thought about what Spude might have been after. Had the hag given Spude some sort of message? Anyway, it didn't matter. This had to be done right. Shadow wasn't going to spend his own blood, not for this.

It was lucky that he had a supply from the children he'd taken. They were more than expendable.

Shadow finished poking at the grave and started scratching an old and powerful and *very evil* symbol into the weathered surface of the headstone.

Nineteen

Howard and Balthazar were waiting. They had been waiting for some time. In fact, they had been waiting on a particular mound of damp earth near and old elm tree for an hour. They had been waiting for an hour for the other idiots (in the snails' opinion) to realise that this is where the trail for the ancient dead bones of a once mighty dragon began.

Oh well, the snails thought. They'll get here eventually…

"We need to find that dragon grave!" Alan muttered as he and the others searched the woods as best they could.

"How big will it be?" Eric asked, not being used to experimental mythological archaeology.

"Depends how much is left," Toad replied, not looking up from the ground.

There is only so long you can wait. Howard and Balthazar looked at each other (in a kind of eye stalks swivelled in arcane manner) and would have nodded it they could be bothered. No one would ever know just how bored snails can get…

Toad didn't notice the two snails until he tripped over Balthazar.

"Sorry," Toad apologised, picking himself up (it's

amazing how even with antennae a snail can glare angrily at someone. Or a toad).

They were all in the woods, trying to find any hint of long dead dragon bones (as you do). Spude hadn't said anything for a while. Eric couldn't decide whether this was because the owl was deep in thought; or his beak had swollen shut with all the rainwater being absorbed into it.

Alan was constantly scanning the ground, stopping now and then to sniff at a random stone or clump of leaves. Toad was still apologising to an angry snail.

"I just didn't see you." He was saying, not realising that Balthazar wasn't listening.

The two snails stopped in front of the companions, blocking their way (if it is even possible for a snail and inch high to impede the progress of anything bigger).

"What?" Alan grunted, completely fed up now. The snails didn't move. Or speak (they don't speak; but adding this brings a bit more drama to the scene).

"I think they want to tell us something," Eric said. The snails seemed to sigh, as if to say: 'at least *this* one's not an idiot'. "What is it?" Eric was sure the snails were twitching their eye stalks. Just slightly…down?

Looking down, Eric couldn't figure out what he was meant to be seeing; mud, leaves, snail mess, small stones, twigs. The others were also looking around the snails now.

"All I see is the slime trail," Alan said, trying to avoid getting his whiskers caught in the goo.

Antennae twitched in irritation.

Toad stuck an inquisitive glare close to the slime and sighed.

"I'm so stupid," he said. The snails looked at each

other. No argument with that statement.

"Right!" An animated Spude suddenly took flight in excitement. "Howard and Balthazar have hit on the right idea! The Snail Trail!"

"O…kay," Eric said, "is this something else I need to learn?"

Spude landed on Eric's shoulder and started his lecture: "The snail trails were used a long time ago to mark the boundaries of ancient burial sites and guide travellers to where they wanted to go."

"Only if they wanted to go to a grave?"

"No. They're a guide."

"Like Snail SAT NAV?"

"Anyway, over time the slime seems to disappear; but it leaves a mark on the earth that can be used by anyone who wants to leave a message or warn someone."

"So…you're saying that snails write with the stuff that comes out of their bottom?" Eric realised that he shouldn't be surprised, as this kind of fact was quickly becoming normal.

Alan looked nervously at the snails. "Well…yes? No one really knows how it works. I mean, the snails don't talk to anyone, do they?" There was no response from the snails. "Do you?" Howard twitched an antenna. He twitched it again. Then he nodded his round head (Eric didn't know if snails actually had 'heads' but it was the end where antennae were and not the end that produces slime / writing tools) in a way that said: 'This Way!'. Then he twitched his eye stalk and in the same direction again, coped by Balthazar. As if to say: 'Yes! Go this way! Why didn't you ask us before?' A smaller twitch 'Idiots'.

"How do we find the snail trail?" Eric asked. *In fact, how do we find and follow a snail trail that might have been left hundreds of years ago?* Eric thought for a moment. "I actually asked that out, didn't I?"

Twenty

Imagine two conkers rolling along the ground at a speed that an average person walks. This is the only way that can describe the movement of the snails as they led the way deeper into the woods.

Eric had learned yet another amazing bit of trivia tonight –snails can actually move very quickly (for them) by curling themselves up into their shells and 'rolling' (although how they knew which way to go when they couldn't see was a mystery. Eric also didn't want to think about the physics of getting and entire snail's squidgy body into a shell that clearly didn't seem big enough. He supposed the 'squidgy' part was important).

"I can't believe we forgot about the snail trails!" Alan grumbled as he padded alongside Eric.

"Even I have to admit that it had slipped my mind," Spude added, "as no one's even talked about the trails for years." It had to be said that even though Spude's mind was an unfathomable mix of knowledge and wisdom, it was still rattling around a collection of twigs, stones, and acorns, with some leaves thrown in.

"How will we know when we find the trail?" Eric asked, trying to walk and search the muddy woods at the same time.

"They'll know," Toad replied into his ear, as he was now sitting on Eric's shoulder due to not being able to keep up. "They'll…er…stop, I suppose." Eric nodded. He'd certainly never read anything about snails using their shells to speed up movement, so finding out that snails have the ability to read long lost trails wasn't as surprising as it would have been a few days ago.

At that moment Howard hit a stone and launched into the air, carried by the speed his shell had been rolling and flying like a rugby ball. There was a 'splosh!" as Howard came down in a puddle. Everyone held their breath (even Spude, who didn't breathe). They watched as a few bubbles popped to the surface of the puddle and a shining shell emerged from the surface of the dirty water, gaining speed until it was clear of the puddle and continuing his way.

Eric wondered how Balthazar had stopped so quickly when Howard went airborne and dive bombed into the puddle but Balthazar sped up again quickly from a standing start and left a groove in the mud and leaves as he followed Howard.

Shadow smiled as he scratched the last symbol into the damp bark of the tree. Not long now – he had all the children he needed, and Alan would not be able to stop him. Shadow laughed, wiping bark that had got stuck to his claw on the wet grass. They wouldn't find him.

Soon he would have an army; he would no longer have to hide in the darkness. Shadow shivered in delight at the thought – not having to change into the shape of a stupid, ridiculous human boy. Being himself. First, he would assemble his army of the dead and hunt down all the animals who had caused problems for him; not just recently, but over the years (it was a *very* long list on vengeance that

Shadow kept in his head).

Shadow allowed himself a small daydream of him sitting on the back of a reanimated dragon that was his to command. He liked it. He liked it a lot; the power, the terror it would cause! And it would look very impressive (looks are important to some people/cats, especially evil geniuses with plans for world domination).

He would gather his allies and start with that graveyard. There would be lots of bodies he could work with and bring them back to some form of life (under his control, of course).

Shadow padded around each of the trees he would use in the ritual; every one of them had a different symbol scratched into the bark by Shadow's claws. Each one had its part to play. Just like the children.

He had to use children – they had more life force in them; it was as simple as that. He didn't like the fact that he had to use so many though. One or two children going missing would not have attracted too much notice. Shadow chuckled to himself.

He thought about the small baby dragon he'd used before to spy on Alan and the boy. If they hadn't gone and used that egg then Shadow would still have his watcher and would know exactly what they were up to.

That baby dragon skeleton had gone now. Shadow had destroyed it by smashing its bones with an unmaking spell. At least the life force he would be using to raise his dragon would be immense and, therefore, magnificent. The magic he would wield!

"What am I looking at?" Eric could only see mud,

leaves, puddles and various other random bits of nature you'd find in woodland. The companions had stopped when Howard and Balthazar slowed down and started going backwards, forwards and side to side like someone who had just got their very first metal detector and was going to prove it was worth the money.

"They've found it," Spude said, swooping down to land by the snails.

"I can't see anything," Eric frowned. Then he blinked and looked again. Still nothing. Earth. He squinted in an effort to make magical snail trails appear.

Alan and Toad were now poking around the patch of mossy grass that the snails were doing criss-cross journeys over.

"It's faint," Toad said.

"Very faint," Alan added, "not seen a trail like this before!"

"I can't see it at all!" Eric felt that everyone else knew something that he didn't (which kind of true, when you think about it), and he wasn't happy about it.

Spude turned his head with a faint sound of rustling leaves. He looked at Eric for a moment.

"Bend down and look at me," the owl ordered, waiting for Eric to do so, "and do...not...blink."

Twenty-One

Eric bent down so that his face was level with Spude and stared straight at the dark oaken eyes.

Spude's beak opened and Eric couldn't describe what came forth. It was a mixture of dust and motes of light, swirling together. Eric could see light blue, yellow, green, all motes of different colour.

He watched mesmerised as Spude's 'breath' travelled along the air and into Eric's eyes.

Then the pain kicked in.

Aaarrrrgghhhhh! Eric screwed his eyes shut as he screamed, trying to block out the agony. He had never experienced pain like it (and he had once eaten an entire box of chocolates that caused him a severe stomach ache). He fell to his knees in the mud and leaves as tears ran down his face.

Eric didn't know how long he stayed like that; it could have been only seconds, but with the pain he felt it was more like days. Eventually, the pain started to lessen, and Eric could open his eyes and be astounded at the new world he was now witness to.

The woods were brighter than before; Eric could see distinct colours of shadow where there used to be just darkness. When he looked at Spude, Eric found that there was a kind of very faint glow around the owl that he hadn't noticed before (Eric assumed this was what people called an 'aura').

Eric also now saw individual hairs in Alan's fur, the different shades in Toad's eyes...and lines. Faint lines in the dirt. They didn't glow or anything; the lines seemed to 'take' colour and light and leave a shape of nothing. It was like looking at a negative of a photograph before the shot had been developed.

The lines were leading away from where he was standing, past the snails and deeper into the woods.

"You see them now." Spude said it wasn't a question. It was a fact. Eric found that he was grinning in spite of the grim situation.

"This is wonderful!" he exclaimed excitedly, "what did you do to my eyes?"

"You have had your human eyes opened to our world," Spude replied seriously, flicking some of the mud that had collected on his wings off into the air.

"But why did it hurt? I mean, that *really* hurt!" Eric said, pointing at his eyes with a shaking finger.

"It has to hurt. The dust gets into your eyes and scratches them so much that the damage is severe. The light gets in your eyes and repairs that damage, as the light has to work on something. But it repairs the eyes better than they ever were before, almost completely new."

"*Damage?*"

"The gift you have been given has been granted to very few humans," Spude replied as though he was ready to move on and wanted to avoid talking about damage.

"Gift? So you deliberately scarred my eyes, then fixed them?" Spude was silent. "You could have explained that before you did it!"

Eric realised that arguing would get him nowhere, especially as, he had to be honest, he had indeed been given this amazing ability. He wondered how long it would last. Even just tonight would be fantastic.

"When will it wear off?" he asked, as the companions followed the now visible tracks.

"It won't," Alan replied before Spude could start another lecture. "You now have this ability forever."

It was time. Shadow began to dig. Down, down; not far. Four paws moving quickly and aided by magic were better than two men with shovels.

Shadow let out a long breath as he gazed at what he had uncovered; dull, very, dark – almost black. It looked like a mixture of wood and bone. Heavy and solid with large holes where gleaming eyes the size of plates used to gaze out at the world from.

With his claws Shadow picked dirt away from large teeth that had not bitten into anything for at least a thousand years; the biggest tooth was a bit large than Shadow's foreleg. And there were lots of teeth.

As he wasn't planning on becoming a dentist for deceased dragons, Shadow ceased his tooth cleaning and used more magic to lift the dragon skull (for that was what it was; if you hadn't figured that out yet, what have you been reading?) out of the compacted damp earth and into the open air for the first time in centuries.

Looking round at the trees surrounding the dragon's grave, Shadow checked that each of the trees had a different symbol again before extending a claw and drawing it swiftly across his chest.

Watching his blood drip onto the dragon skull, Shadow allowed himself a smile as the dark liquid was absorbed into the ancient bone.

A glow, faint, appeared behind the monstrous eye sockets.

"It starts now…"

Twenty-Two

It was getting colder. Eric shivered. His knees were still damp from when he had experienced the 'gift' of getting new sight (in a painful way). Eric had to admit that despite the agonising way he was given it, the sight was *amazing*. As he got used to it, Eric was able to follow the ancient snail trails quite easily, even sometimes pointing them out to the others, who hadn't noticed them.

"You've a talent for this," Toad commented, "finding the snail trails."

Eric was grinning as he replied, "Robin will never believe this. He'll think I'm some superhero." Eric thought for a moment. "Although, he does wear glasses." Eric chuckled. "He'd love this." The happy feeling drained away, replaced by the memory of seeing his best friend rendered helpless by a shape-shifting cat and dragged into a school locker.

"You'll find him." Toad said, noticing Eric's sudden change of mood and correctly guessing what had caused it. Eric found he was touched by Toad's concern. He did something he'd never ever thought he would do. Eric bent down and held his hand out for Toad to high-five him. Toad did so, grinning.

"Team Robin," Toad said, holding his foreleg tenderly as he had high-fived Eric's outstretched hand a bit too hard…

Shadow gazed up at the night sky, exhausted. He didn't know how much of his blood had been used in the ritual but was sure that it had been worth it.

On shaking legs, Shadow slowly picked himself up and looked around in a tired daze. He smiled. Tottering on weak limbs, Shadow walked over to the nearest tree that had been used in the ritual. Gazing up at the symbol he had carved, Shadow's smile grew broader as he could feel his triumph getting closer. His nose twitched as he could smell the blood that was now lazily seeping out of the symbol and down the bark of the tree.

His strength returning quickly, Shadow paced around to every tree an noticed the same thing. Each tree he had used in the ritual was now leaking blood from a symbol carved into the reddening bark.

Shadow wiped his nose with the back of his paw, smearing part of the blood that had come out of it across his muzzle. It made his nose colder in the night air.

A crunching noise behind him made Shadow turn. Looking up, then looking up some more, he smiled in horrible satisfaction at the towering monster in front of him.

They found the ritual site by accident.

To be more accurate, Toad had an accident by not looking where he was going and falling into a big hole. It was obvious that *something* had been down there, buried in the earth. Dead. Rotting.

Eric helped Toad out of the hole (which on the evidence had been made by furious but determined digging – it was clear that someone *really* wanted what was here) as Alan and Spude looked around in horror. The trail had led to this spot. All the companions wished that it hadn't.

Surrounding the dig site there was a tightly packed circle of trees. But these trees were like nothing Eric had ever seen before. Carved into each tree was a symbol – all of them different and they made his newly – upgraded eyes hurt and blur a bit as he looked at them.

The horrible bit was the blood. It was pooling at the bottom of each tree and had seeped out of the carved symbol, as if the carving had made the trees bleed.

"No…" Alan sat on the muddy ground, head down. Toad joined him. The snails rolled around the trees, not really noticing (or seeming to care) that they were making new trails with the blood they had cruised through.

"I'm sorry Eric," Toad said, sorrow filling his eyes as Eric looked at him in puzzlement. "This is the vilest, nastiest thing I've ever seen." A prickle of worry began creeping its way up Eric's spine. "I didn't think he'd go this far."

Eric glanced at Spude for an explanation. The owl seemed to sag in defeat.

"Look into the trees," Spude instructed.

"How?"

"Your eyes will see beyond the outer screen of the world if you need them to, even though you won't like what you see."

Eric found the nearest tree, fearful of what he might find. If he concentrated, Eric realised that the layers of bark and wood appeared transparent. It was like something viewed through a glass bottle in dim sunlight. What he saw made him cry out in alarm and fall to his knees for the second time that night.

He was sick.

It was disgusting. Horrible. Toad, managing to avoid Eric's small puddle of vomit, stood next to the boy and put a stubby foreleg on his arm in sympathy.

Eric composed himself and looked up again.

Within the tree was something with pale, greyish-white skin. It had sunken cheeks and looked as though it hadn't eaten for a very long time. It was the eyes though that Eric would never forget.

Staring, lifeless, looking out on nothing, faintly tinged with a red haze. The eyes that would forever remain in Eric's memory.

Tear welled up and down Eric's cheeks again, although for entirely different reasons than getting his 'gift'.

Encased within the tree was one of Eric's classmates. One of the missing children from school.

Penny.

Twenty-Three

Howard and Balthazar let the boy absorb the horror of what he had seen. They admitted to each other (through a series of eye twitches) that this turn of events wasn't exactly what they had expected. The question was, what to do about it?

They glanced at each other again. It was time. It was time to do something they hadn't done in a very long time.

It was time to fight...

Every tree contained a child from Eric's school, including Robin. Eric had no tears left. Wiping his eyes with his sleeve, he looked at Alan, Spude and Toad with a fierce expression.

"I'm going to kill him." Eric's voice grated through gritted teeth. "No one's going to believe any of this. Shadow's killed my friends."

Alan shook his head sadly. "No. You're too good for that. If you take the life of anything, even a creature as evil as Shadow, then you'll just be as bad as him."

"Then what can I do?" Eric yelled, not caring who or what heard him.

"We may be able to restore them," Spude said, flapping in front of Eric quickly as if to bar his way.

"Of course!" Toad slapped his foreleg on his head (which looks ridiculous; and would have been hysterically funny if it weren't for the scene of blood and death). "As long as the blood is flowing the ritual isn't finished! If we can find Shadow we could reverse the spell!"

"An Unmaking Spell!" Alan agreed, nodding enthusiastically.

Eric felt his spirits lift a little.

"Where do we find Shadow?"

There was a slight tremor in the ground under Eric's feet. And he could hear a crunching, 'splat' sound coming closer as though someone was pressing gravel into wet sand.

"Er…" Toad said slowly, prodding Eric so he turned to see what Toad was looking at.

And then hell broke loose.

Alan lost it. There was no other explanation. Rage didn't describe what he was feeling. Bunching up his muscles the big powerful cat charged, shouting at the top of his voice. He didn't see anything but Shadow. He didn't see what smashed into him with so much force he was flung backwards into a tree, splintering bark with the energy of the impact.

Alan's vision blurred. He could taste blood in his mouth and his chest was stinging as though a thousand bees had made a nest there and got really angry. A veteran of fights for hundreds of years, Alan was sure that some of his ribs were cracked.

This wasn't in anything that Eric had EVER read. The thing in front of him in its monstrous glory wouldn't make sense in any science book. Part of his mind was almost trying to deny what he was seeing, and Eric felt that even without his new visual ability he would be able to witness the horror before him.

A massive, distorted skull with glowing blue light emanating from its eye sockets, elongated snout and jaw furnished with large teeth. A short neck like a gorilla's led from the skull to an immense ribcage and spine; all the vertebrae picked out in sharp, age-blackened bone.

Forelegs and back legs like tree trunks ending in heavy feet and claws; ridiculously big footprints were left in the soft ground. For some reason Eric's brain registered the fact that the footprint he'd seen when he'd thrown the egg was just like this – except that this was like comparing the size of a vulture to a sparrow.

The body led to a long tail that just seemed to be an extension of the spine. This tail ended in a big bone shaped like a hammer. All blackened bone and ghostly light.

It was the wings though. The wings were what slammed Eric's senses out of his head for a moment so that he couldn't think. Imagine a bat's wings, elongated bone reaching out to create a wingspan wider than two houses put together. In place of skin stretching across the frame of bone to complete the wings was a smoky, fuzzy blue light, like a blue torch shone underwater and looked at from above the surface.

And sitting atop the massive skull. A cat. A big black cat with half of its ear missing.

Eric was shocked out of his fear by Alan yelling loudly and charging at the immense beast. Eric winced as the undead dragon swung its hammer like tail and caught Alan right in the chest, launching the heroic cat through the air to come crashing into a tree. Eric though his heart stopped before he noticed that Alan was moving. Hurt, and probably badly, but still moving.

"You …brat." A voice that scratched at Eric's brain came at him. "You interfering insect…"

Twenty-Four

So – this was Shadow. The *real* Shadow. A voice like chisels being pounded into stone. If he was honest, Eric thought Shadow's voice would be higher, more like nails scratching glass. Gathering all his courage, Eric looked straight at the evil cat, managing to avoid glancing at the skeletal dragon.

"Eric," he said evenly and slowly. "My name is *Eric*."

Shadow grinned.

"It doesn't matter," Shadow replied coolly, just before the skull of the dragon opened its jaws and let forth a stream of white fire.

Eric jumped to the side as the flames hit the ground where he had been and incinerated a fallen log. Cinders and minute scraps of burning wood flew everywhere. Spude had to fly high to avoid being set alight as Toad dived behind a tree (then thought better of it as he had taken cover from flames behind something made of wood).

Eric shook his head to clear it. By jumping out of the way of the flames he had gone straight to the ground and landed on his elbow in a funny way. More pain to add to his night. Making him dizzy. He could move everything so Eric didn't think it was broke. Deep down, Eric knew that he was out of his depth. All his books wouldn't help him now.

Eric looked up just as the reanimated dragon stalked towards him with slow, deliberate strides, each step causing a small cascade of mud and dirt circling around the monster's skeletal feet.

The deformed head stretched down at Eric, casting everything around him in the ghostly light from its eyes. By now, Eric had got to one knee, supporting his elbow on his leg. He felt something in his pocket. It was not quite round, and like a big pebble. Eric suddenly realised what he had.

An egg!

The massive jaws opened again; and Eric couldn't help catching sight of Shadow's gloating face, made even more demonic by the light.

Fingers in his pocket, Eric closed them around the egg, muscles and elbow screaming at him in pain. The first rush of flame started building up in the dragon's mouth.

Eric moved.

Just before the flame erupted, Eric brought his hand up quickly and slammed the egg hard on the side of the dragon's face.

There was a scream that split Eric's eardrums and sent him back to the floor. He'd hurt a dragon! And for some reason he couldn't help thinking that he now had smashed egg on his hand!

Somewhere in the dragon's reanimated cold mind it sensed something. A feeling. Pain. It reared its massive skull back, taking Shadow with it and throwing the evil cat clear into the trees. Eric saw a glowing 'splotch' mark in the shape of his hand on the dragon's face, fading down to a black deeper than the bone it was burning into.

Then the dragon raised its foot and would have squashed Eric into the mud if two shapes hadn't whizzed out of nowhere and hit the ankle, staggering the dragon.

They landed one each side of Eric, from spinning to a stop in less than a heartbeat.

Howard and Balthazar looked at Eric intently (some would say the snails were slightly impressed by Eric's heroism, but let's be honest, we'll never know). Eric realised at that moment that the age-old facts about snails being slow were all lies. They can be fast. Very fast. They just don't show off. (They certainly don't let one that they can spin extremely fast at about cyclone speeds and propel themselves as miniature tactical weapons). Eric couldn't be sure, but he thought that both snails *nodded* to him before starting to spin again, as Toad finally got out of cover and ran over.

The dragon looked down at the companions, seeming confused, before starting forwards again, still intent on turning Eric into the World's Flattest Boy.

Two things happened; firstly, Balthazar succeeded in hitting the dragon again, this time right on the nose. Secondly, Howard also hit the dragon on the chest and rebounded back right into Toad, who was flung sideways and down into the hole that he had fallen into before, with Howard landing on top of him.

Using this as a distraction, Eric clambered up on aching legs and ran into the trees, frantically looking for Spude. As though by magic, Spude landed before him, out of sight (but they suspected not for long) of the dragon.

"What do we do?" Eric almost shouted, feeling his throat hurt with the effort.

Spude looked at Eric and then down at his twig feet. He blinked. Then the owl faced Eric with determined but encouraging gaze (and definitely a wooden gaze).

"You'll know what to do," the owl said kindly, "remember, you're the grandson of Mother Cerridwen."

"What?"

"Let the words come, I believe in you. We all believe in you." With that, Spude took to the air with a flap of leafy wings and flew straight at the dragon.

"Spude!" Eric yelled, "The flames!"

"The unmaking spell!" Spude called back as he zigzagged around the dragon's head, causing the undead monster to follow him and try to catch the owl in its gaping flame-wreathed mouth.

Eric saw Balthazar rolling forward again, building up speed for another assault.

Gritting his teeth, Eric stepped out from the trees. *What was he meant to say?* He knew Spude and Balthazar were risking themselves to distract the dragon while Eric came up with this spell that they all believed he knew.

Not looking where he was going, Eric slipped in some of the blood still pooling around one of the trees. Putting his hand out on the trunk to steady himself, Eric brushed against the bloodied symbol carved there.

And he knew.

Twenty-Five

It flooded into his mind like a tsunami, building up in waves of unimagined depth ready to be let out.

As though in a trance, Eric walked forwards, directly at the dragon and his remaining friends still battling it.

From Nowhere To Here
False Light Taken
Give Back To Light
All That Forsaken

Eric froze. Everything else seemed to move lightning quick. The dragon stopped suddenly, shaking, before the light in its eyes and surrounding its wings shut off dramatically and the entire skeleton (now lifeless again) collapsed.

Looking around, Eric saw the blood that had pooled at the base of the trees start to move – no, crawl back up the bark and be absorbed into the symbol cut into each one.

Then nothing.

Time kicked in for Eric again like a bell being struck with a large hammer. The dragon was a pile (a BIG pile) of blackened bone, the palm print from Eric's egg attack still etched into the skull.

Balthazar slowly rolled over to Eric, emerging from under the rib cage of the fallen monster. Eric breathed out.

Then thought. Something was wrong. Then he noticed it.

Gently spiralling down to settle on the bones of the dragon were fragments of bark, leaves and two longer twigs. Eric closed his eyes. The unmaking spell.

Spude was gone.

"Did...we...win?" A very faint voice rose from the hole as a snail popped up over the edge. Eric turned round and was about to say how amazing it was that Howard had finally spoken before he remembered that Toad was still down there.

"The dragon's gone," Eric replied, still not sure what to feel, as even though they had beaten the dragon they had still lost their wooden owl. Eric bent over the hole and picked up the prone amphibian, who had landed on his head and had gone an inch into the earth so that his eyes were covered, and the soil almost touched his mouth. Toad shook the dirt off and looked blearily at Eric. He nodded.

"Told you," he said, "team Robin." Then Toad noticed Eric's expression. "What is it?" Eric took him over to the dragon bones and the components of Spude that were lying on it like sugar dusted on a dessert. "Oh," Toad sighed, blinking, "I wasn't expecting that." It was all quiet for a moment. There wasn't even any breeze. It was as though the world had decided to give the friends a brief moment to mourn the loss of their owl.

The group was completed by Alan dragging himself across the ground to join them. Wheezing, bleeding, tired, but alive.

"I'll live," he stated as the others looked at him. Alan took a few more deep, ragged breaths. "What happened to

Shadow?"

Eric's head snapped round to where the evil cat had been thrown when the dragon recoiled in pain. What he saw was horrible yet satisfying, in a grim way. Putting Toad down, Eric then picked up the injured Alan and together the group walked slowly to where Eric was looking.

Shadow's blood dribbled down the tree. He was there, head slumped onto his chest, legs slack at his side, eyes closed.

A massive branch was sticking out of his chest. It had entered his back and exited the front as Shadow had flown through the air and got himself impaled.

Now he wasn't moving at all.

Dead.

No one said anything. There was nothing to say.

They put the dragon's bones back into the hole from whence it came. Spude's various components were added as the companions pushed the dirt and soil back over the remains. Breathing hard with the effort, Eric stood up and looked at the trees around the grave.

The blood had gone now (well mostly), and the bark on most of the trees had dried. Even the carved symbols had disappeared from all but one of the trees.

Eric walked over to the nearest tree and using his new vision looked inside. It was Robin!

Twenty-Six

The boy looked healthy, not pale and bloodless like Penny had done. That was good. Hopefully, it meant that the ritual had been reversed in full. But how could they get the children out of the trees?

Eric put his hand out to touch the bark, hesitating for only a second before he admitted what he was afraid of; Eric was about to try and being his best friend back and hadn't any idea what he would do if it didn't work.

Eric's hand pressed against the bark. For some reason, he knew this was the right thing to do without knowing why. *Was this more of what Spude had been talking about?* Eric wondered, as he felt the rough surface tremble!

Snatching his hand back quickly, Eric stepped away from the tree as the bark peeled back like a snake shedding skin and Robin's body was pushed out of the tree.

Toad rushed over to the boy on the ground and put a stubby finger to Robin's head. "He's alive," Toad announced, nodding happily (but also relieved). "He'll wake up soon."

Eric grinned. Then he realised that everyone was now looking at him. Expecting.

"What?" he asked. Alan sighed.

"The others," Alan pointed to the trees in exasperation, "get the other children out!"

Ah. Right. Eric had been so caught up in finding and

freeing Robin that he had forgotten about the other captives. Guilt made him act quickly. It was the same process for all the other trees.

Until Eric finally came to the tree where Penny was entombed. He stopped as his breath caught.

Where all the other children now looked healthy and unhurt (just sleeping), Penny was exactly the same as she had been when Eric had first discovered her in the tree.

She may as well have been dead...

The official story (and this also ended up in the newspapers and on the news in the evening) was that the missing children had all been found asleep in a quiet part of the woods by a local schoolboy who had been 'out walking'.

Eric said that his elbow injury was from 'tripping up' in the darkness. No one asked why Eric had been out in the woods so late at night. After being interviewed by a reporter, Eric was then spoken to by the police, who were the same officers that Eric had seen at Robin's. Also a 'Detective' who asked for details about the event and in particular if Eric knew anything about a girl from his class called Penny who so far was still missing.

It was all a blur to Eric. If he had been honest with the adults then he would have had to explain why when he came back to the scene with his parents Eric had not seen anything of Penny. The tree that had encased her was empty; the symbol carved into the bark was, however faint, still there.

The friends didn't say much to each other for a few days

afterwards (Howard and Balthazar didn't say anything). Eric had let Alan climb into his lap a lot more than usual to be stroked and fussed over. Toad hadn't touched a cheese sandwich for a day and a half (everyone thought he might be ill).

Robin and his parents came round to thank Eric; an event that was repeated several times as parents showed their gratitude. A couple brought cakes. One parent had bought Eric a book token (Eric's love of reading was legendary).

Eric found that he didn't want to talk about what had happened. He nodded and mumbled something about 'anyone would have done the same' which people seemed to accept. It was really difficult when Penny's father visited and said that Eric had done a great thing and even though Penny was still missing Eric was a hero.

School was even worse. The entire school, including the pupils, teachers, caretaker and dinner ladies all welcomed Eric with a cheer. It was starting to annoy him. He hadn't rescued Penny. He'd found her, but not been able to do anything; this upset and frustrated Eric more than anything. Why not Penny? Eric knew that he should let this go; he had done a good thing, overall. But part of him still felt like a failure.

At least no one was asking about Shane, who had also disappeared. No one seemed to care though, and Eric hoped it stayed that way.

He also hoped no one went digging around the site for evidence; it wasn't the possibility of someone discovering dragon bones. Eric didn't want Spude's remains (even though they weren't his 'true' remains) to be disturbed.

Eric did manage to pluck up the courage to ask his parents about his grandmother. Over dinner he had asked a seemingly innocent question about Grandma liking animals. Eric felt that the answers came a bit too quickly and with startled looks. They wouldn't go into detail. Eric didn't mind. At that point, he could wait. He knew deep down that he would be able to figure out the truth. Eric knew he could ask Toad and Alan for advice (obviously not the snails).

What was really hard was hiding his new vision. It was the fact that he now noticed things he hadn't before; a mouse scampered out of the shadows at school and Eric jumped at the sudden scare. However, he had seen the mouse a couple of second before his classmates and so Eric reacted in a way they thought 'odd'.

There were times when Eric wanted to tell Robin everything. But he couldn't. First of all, Robin would get far too excited and insist on meeting all the animals, and secondly, Robin could not be trusted to keep his mouth shut. Secrecy, as difficult as it was going to be, seemed the best option.

Eric did wonder though what else he didn't know about the world of animals he had been let into.

He closed his bedroom curtains and got into bed, Alan curling up beside him and Toad nestling on a cushion under the bed...

Epilogue

Eyes with a red hue to them watched Eric close his bedroom curtains and disappear into the safety of his dreams.

Pale hands with chipped nails gripped the branch firmly, using it to steady their hold before the short drop to the ground.

Dirty blonde hair shone briefly in the moonlight before disappearing into the trees as Eric's bedroom light went out and the garden was plunged into darkness…